INK MOVEMENT'S

MISSISSAUGA YOUTH ANTHOLOGY:

VOLUME III

Mississauga Youth Anthology Volume III

Compiled by: Cynthia Feng

Editors: Amy Kwong
Sadia Sheikh
Kathy Hu
Sarena Daljeet
Ahmad Younes
Tanisha Mehta

Publisher: In Our Words Inc./inourwords.ca

Cover Design: Jessica Feng
Tahreem Alvi

Book Design: Shirley Aguinaldo

Library and Archives Canada Cataloguing in Publication

Ink Movement's Mississauga youth anthology. Volume III / compiled by Cynthia Feng ; editors, Amy Kwong, Sadia Sheikh, Kathy Hu, Sarena Daljeet, Ahmad Younes, Tanisha Mehta.

ISBN 978-1-926926-51-3 (paperback)

1. Youths' writings, Canadian (English)--Ontario--Mississauga. 2. Canadian poetry (English)--Ontario--Mississauga. 3. Short stories, Canadian (English)--Ontario--Mississauga. 4. Canadian poetry (English)--21st century. 5. Canadian fiction (English)--21st century. I. Feng, Cynthia, 1997-, compiler II. Ink Movement, organizer III. Title: Mississauga youth anthology.

PS8235.Y6I66 2015 C810.8'09283 C2015-904053-1

INTRODUCTION

Dear Reader,

Thank you for picking up a copy of the *Mississauga Youth Anthology: Volume III*. The Ink Movement Mississauga team has put an immense effort into this publication over the past few months, and we couldn't be more thrilled to be presenting you the finalized book.

This year, we received over 200 extremely diverse submissions for the anthology, covering a wide range of art forms, ideas, topics and styles. Our team spent weeks selecting the works and arranging them into our three-part theme: dreams, nostalgia, and regret. As you flip through the writing, artwork, and photography in the pages before you, we hope you reflect and resonate with the stories our contributors have captured.

To all the talented local youth who have contributed to this publication: thank you for sharing your stories, passions and art with us. To all the community partners who have made this publication possible: thank you for allowing us to provide these youth with a platform for their art. To my Ink Movement team: thank you for your tireless dedication to making this project a success.

So, reader, I hope you enjoy reading this anthology in the best way you know how, whether that means you're snuggled in bed or lying on the floor, sipping coffee or tea, reading it cover to cover or skimming over random pages.

On behalf of the entire Ink Movement team, thank you for your support to our project and to your local youth.

Stay 'ink'spired.

Much love,

Cynthia Feng

President, Ink Movement Mississauga

Dear Reader,

How often is it that you think to the future, to the days when your dreams come true, to the years when everything will be within your reach?

How often is it that you think to the past, to the nostalgia of your childhood, to the joy of a thousand stories told?

How often is it that you think to your choices, to what you've done, to what you wish you did?

The book that you hold in your hand is a collection of those very thoughts: the dreams, nostalgias, and regrets of the youth in Mississauga. Today, they share their stories with you, whether it be through prose, poetry, photography, or art. I sincerely hope that through this anthology, you will meet something new, something that touches you and leads you to inspiration.

Finally, I would like to thank you, readers, for opening these pages and helping to make our dreams come true.

So, dear readers, never stop dreaming.

Amy Kwong

Youth Anthology Lead, Ink Movement Mississauga

Dear Reader,

It has become a clichéd statement, yet it remains true: Youth are often not given a voice—in politics, in education, in literature. I founded Ink Movement three years ago because I recognized that youth have important stories to tell. Financial and other barriers to publishing should not stand in the way of that. The Mississauga Youth Anthology became Ink Movement's signature project because it provides an outlet for youth to share their stories in the form of poetry, short stories (obviously), essays, visual art, and photography. The anthology series celebrates creative expression, artistry, and voices that may not otherwise be acknowledged in literature.

I am proud to present the third instalment of the Mississauga Youth Anthology for your reading pleasure. Every year, I take another step away from the project, as will have to be the case for the anthology series to be truly sustainable over the long run. I am incredibly grateful for the people who have stepped in as I have stepped away, devoting hours of their efforts to support a vision that unites us. In particular, thank you to Cynthia Feng, Tina Chu, Amy Kwong, the wonderful editorial and graphic design teams, and everyone at Ink Movement Mississauga. Last but not least, thank you to all of the contributors for lending your stories to this book, and thank you, dear reader, for providing a home for these stories.

Maxwell Tran

Founder and Executive Director, Ink Movement Mississauga

TABLE OF CONTENTS

Poems/Stories, *Illustrations*

RENA GAO

I AM A WRITER

I am a writer.
You may call me a time-waster
Or a collector of useless things.
But in reality I am a collector
of beautiful things.
I weave my words and
carefully set them free
from the confines of my mind.
I am a fisherman;
I create a net of sentences,
and string them into one.
Then I wave it in the water
and catch the wandering souls–
the souls with colours that match my own.
I am a painter of all things lost.
I bring them to life with a stroke of the brush.
I draw with the colours of the heavens
So that you will cry when you touch them
Or when they touch you.
I am the finale of a play,
When the masks come off
and the tears come on,
I inspire and I write.
I am the mirror that hangs on your boudoir,
I display the beauty of your soul.
I am whatever you desire me to be
A dream, a cry from a faraway land,
an ocean of grief,
of joy, of beauty.
I am just a girl, but I am a writer.
I write to live, and I live to write.
My life is a canvas, one that begs to be filled.
So if you see me with a blank, faraway look in my eyes,
I am feeding my soul.

JACQUELINE SHI

THE WORLDLY VOYAGE

MAHEK SHERGILL

HOME - BIRTH OF HOPE

My mother held me in the cusps of her rough hands,
like I was 7 pounds of gold
instead of flesh.
In the rugged graveyard of her hands,
a reason for religion.

Oh, the foxes are familiar with her taste,
their tenacious paws etching galaxies of crimson
in the ridges of her hips.
She is nothing
but the remains of hungry lust.

She had never known colours,
like the ones that the sunset unveiled,
oh so slowly,
that night.
She had never known bliss,
like the rise and fall of my chest
oh so slowly,
that night.

In the midst of time,
we lay still for what seemed like days or hours.

To her,
my cheeks are nothing less
than the velvet poppies lining Flanders Fields.
To her,
I am the hopeful sprouts around Hiroshima.

In the dark emptiness between my little fingers,
her rough hands have found belonging.
In the soundlessness of that night
my love for her was silent but deep

like an ocean at dusk.
And she drowned herself in it

And finally found home in me.

NASHWA KHAN AND HANA SHAFI

POETRY

"Remember your roots," they say,
difficult when your homeland regurgitated to you,
fed back through white filters.

"Stay rooted," they echo,
impossible while you flip through pages of books,
bleached content like its pages.

"Stay grounded, " they croon,
over the phone from back home,
a home I don't seem to know.

Uprooted.
Transplanted.
But not all transplants take.

Two Feet,
Planted,
No Where.

KATHRYN CHUNG

WHAT PHYSICS

CINDY LIN

THE COSMOS

It is 3 AM, and I can't stop thinking about how lovely the stardust looks floating around the corners of my lonely room, how my sweat is entangled with love I had lost many nights ago under my sheets, my sore limbs aching to feel something, anything, to distract my destructive mind from the emptiness in my chest. Everything is so frighteningly real, so strange, and you realize that this is it; this is now; this is what my bones have been lusting for in third grade. I remember the summer nights spent with dandelions in my hand, and the sun so painfully bright in my youthful eyes, and the wind so beautifully wild in my hair. I may have been lost, but there was not a single care in the cosmos, and I ruled my own world with love as a child of the galaxy. Now there is a black hole sucking out my soul, and I can't seem to figure it out; nobody seems to be able to figure it out. The shooting star will pass soon, my love.

NEHA NAEEM

DRIFTING IN A SERENE REALITY

JANE WANG

A CANDID INTERVIEW WITH THE SELF AT 11:48 PM

A: We're recording. So, tell everyone a little bit about yourself.

B: You know, it's questions like these that I hate the most. I don't know who I am. You remember how at the beginning of every single year from kindergarten to middle school, your teachers would ask you to create a little something that represented who you are? I'd always be stumped. My friends would all draw things like soccer balls and flowers and ice cream and their pets and I'd draw things that I liked too, but isn't it weird to use things you like to represent who you are? There's so much more to you than that.

A: I kind of get it. But you also sound a little pretentious.

B: Yeah, sorry. I haven't slept more than twenty hours this week. I'm running on sheer willpower alone. You'll have to excuse me if I don't make any sense. You caught me at a bad time.

A: That's tough. We'll get straight to it, then: tell us about your plans for the future. What are you going to do?

B: Right now I *really* want to be an engineer. I want to drown myself in math. I applied to [redacted] and [redacted], and I really, really want to get into [redacted]. I'm going to graduate with job experience, get picked up by a company in my fourth year, graduate, and start living the dream.

A: Wow. That's pretty concrete.

B: Yeah. But then again, is that what I really want to do? I'm not completely sure. Have I told you about my Character Theory?

A: No, not yet. Shoot.

B: Okay. First, it's not really a theory. At least, not in the scientific sense. I just gave it a name to make it sound Cool and Important.

A: Okay. No harm done.

B: Alright. Well, what if throughout the course of my life, I have the possibility of becoming, say, one thousand different people? Like, if circumstances had been just the littlest bit different, I would have become a completely different person. And right now, I'm only on five hundred or so. I'm only [redacted]! I'm still young! I can say with certainty that this is what I want to do now, but how do I know I'm making the right choice? I could be a completely different person in ten years.

A: What do you mean? Won't you still be the same person?

B: No, I'd be a different person. What I may choose will change me into a different person.

A: But even if you choose things that are inconsistent with the you of right now, you'll still be you no matter what you choose. We don't change, we only become more of what we are. The you that is evolving will change what you choose.

B: I suppose that's one way of looking at it. But then what drives your evolution?

A: I don't know. Your environment? Any new information you receive? The opinions of others? But choices, in my opinion, aren't what changes us. They're more like the products of our change.

B: Yeah. That makes sense, I guess.

A: So going back to your original question...I guess we don't know if we're ever making the right choices. So many things could happen between this point and some distant point in the future that it's almost impossible to guess what might happen.

B: So what should I do? Just believe that I'm right and guess the rest along the way?

A: Yeah. What else can you do?

B: ...Talking with you never yields anything not anti-climactic, does it.

A: Hey, you're me, too.

[there is a short lull in the conversation]

B: All this introspection made me tired.

A: Good night.

B: Good night.

ERICA YARMOL-MATUSIAK

IS THE WATER BRIGHTER ON THE FLIPSIDE

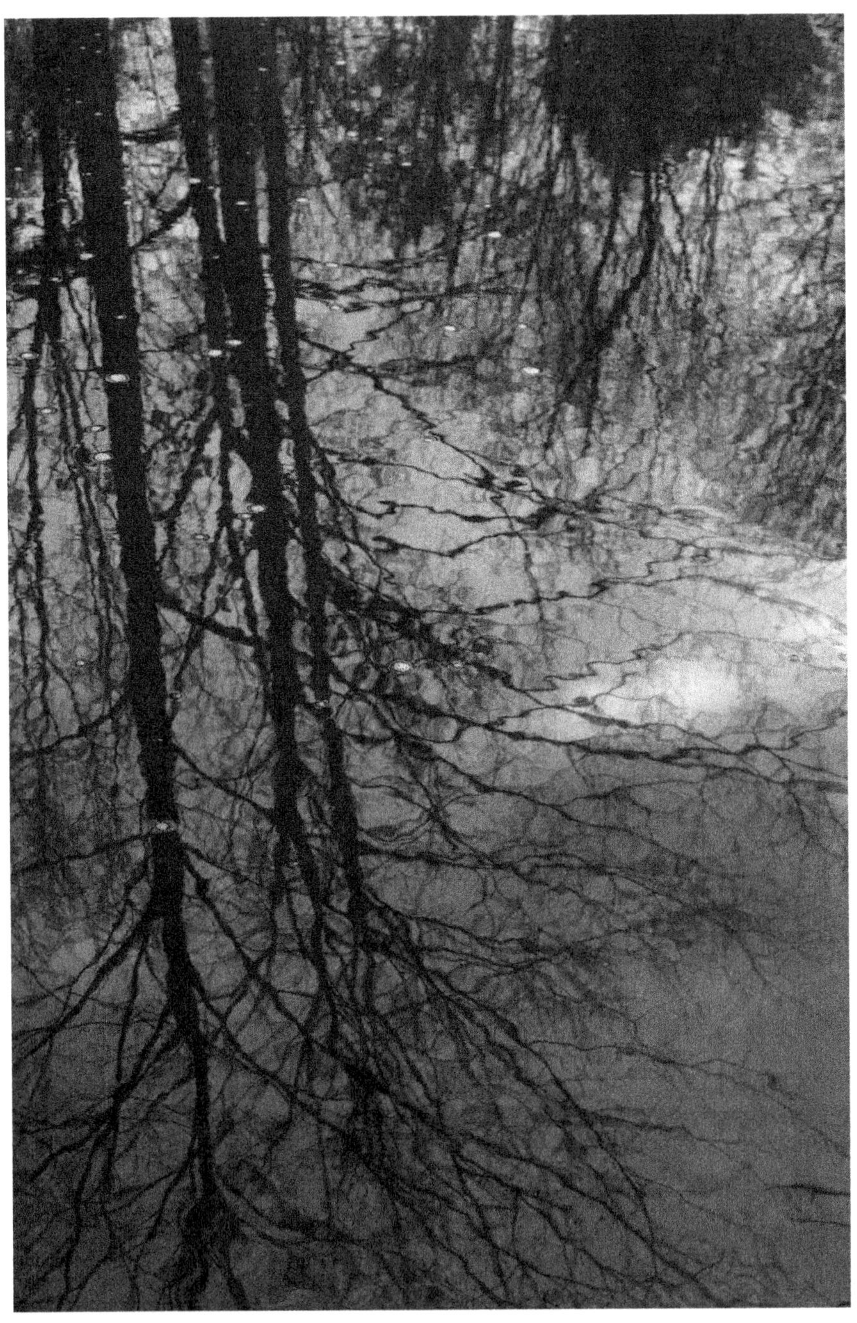

SADIA SHEIKH

UNRAVEL THE WORLD

You are young
and there is more at work here
than your lungs.
Untainted,
fate's intrigue will leave you wanton
the same hands you walked on
your chains.

Grass in the restless wind
blades between your fingers
a heart each in your mouths
held hands coughing up blood.

Here, vomit within
tongue cut on teeth
control will have you suck
swallow
the
spit at your feet.

Kisses from curiosity
drew bite marks on your pencils
stretch marks on your thighs
warmer lips than you have veins
he'll leave you a girl
from the waist
down.

Angels in the snow
three legs in a race weren't enough
to keep you walking
straight
a gunshot for every sprint
bones fused at the babe's wake

polished, at the end
to the earth's taste.

Nature, the striptease,
has already stripped you
naked.

PRASIDDHA PARTHASARATHY

MAGIC OF MY OWN

I was 100% sure my eleventh birthday would present the greatest gift of all:
my letter of acceptance to Hogwarts.
I'm 16 now.
I've concocted all the ways my letter may have gotten lost:
Stuck, trapped, interfered, hidden, misplaced.
Consumed, stolen, torn — some act of distaste!
But in the five years since, my owl should have made it, right?
Despite this, in my years of waiting, a few lessons I have noted.
Gryffindors, I have seen.
These people in my life with the hearts of lions, their strength of character so fortifying.
These scintillating souls are marked by the insignia of imminent greatness.
And of course, I meet Hufflepuffs everyday; I laugh with these kindred spirits whose laughter, like babes, deem nonexistent all the pain of the world.
Now, not to forget, many of my kin are Ravenclaws: master wielders of knowledge, whose wise minds propel our world forward.
And I can't forget the Slytherins in my life, eyes brimming with potential, profundity at their fingertips. Fleeting differences with the Slytherins motivate me to try harder and change my game.
Sufficed to say, I'm starting to think I may just be living in my own Hogwarts.
And that, my dear wizards, is swell.

RENEE VETTIVELU

AERIAL ALPS

MICHELLE MA

HEART OF MY HEART

7.
You light a cigarette while I stare, and when the ashes fall, you dust them away with your foot and chuckle. I watch the smoke come out in puffs, spilling out your lips.
You catch my gaze. "What?"
"It's raining," I say. And it is – the rain drums an inconsistent rhythm on the asphalt. Our clothes are damp and your zipper is undone. My palms are clammy, fingers cold.
"I know."
You bring it to your lips and I'm still watching. The words from your mouth die and then rise.

6.
When you were seven, you stole your mother's stamps and coated your skin with the Canadian flag. The adults laughed when they saw you, and the rest of us thought you were weird, but you still thought you could be shipped away.

5.
You were the one who told me that we were all strays searching for homes in each other.
"Have you found one yet?" I asked.
You shrugged, mouth curled up in a half-frown. "There's no point in leaving the chrysalis if you've got no desire to fly, y'know."
"Then what about me?"
You looked at me and scowled. "How am I supposed to know that?"
You didn't then, and you still don't. Even now, you're looking for a place to belong.
I guess, so am I.

4.
In a desperate attempt to fit a thousand lives into your own, you ran. No one was prepared for that.

3.
"... Why are you here?"
"Iis there a reason I can't be here?"
"You were gone."
"I know."
"You were supposed to have left."
"I know that, too."
"So why didn't you just stay away?"
"They say home is where the heart is. And well, I've only ever had one of those."
Pause.
"You're an idiot."
You laugh. "I know," you say, "I know."

2.
I step over the cracks in the sidewalk, hands out to balance myself. You follow, a few strides behind. Your sneakers are new but your laces are already dirty. You're holding a cup of black coffee, strong enough to keep your heart alive and beating. Ribs aren't cages, and I'm no longer at the front door of your heart, screaming to be let in.
"Hey."
I turn. "What?"
Your smile is wide and your fingers aren't trembling any more. You open your mouth to say something and I think, maybe this is all that matters.

1.
This weather, it will last for good.

JANE JOMY

PERSPECTIVE

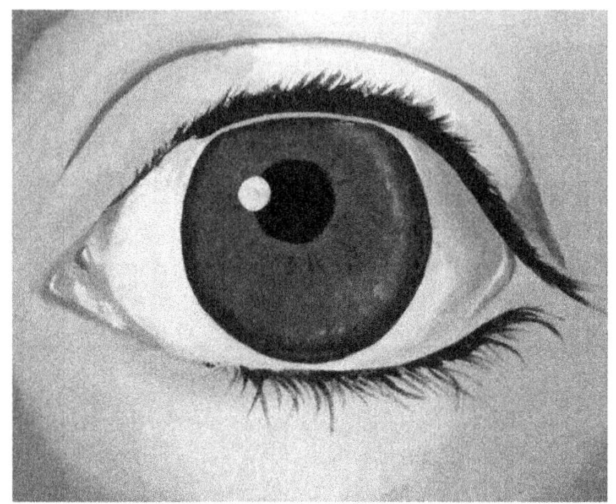

JORDAN CURRIE

FANCIFUL

When we're children, we're told that dreams are something
you only experience in sleep.
Our minds are too fragile, too small,
to capture all the shouting voices
telling us what and what not to believe.
We sleep, and we're there,
in a dream that's far too fanciful for us to process.
You could be floating on a cloud, swimming in nectar,
facing your biggest fear.

Fast forward a few years.
Dreams are no longer something we greet in slumber.
They're something shoved at you,
something you must choose rather than being chosen by it.
At least, that's what they tell us.

They don't tell you that some dreams are more practical than others
until it's too late.
You're envious of the lucky ones,
the kids who know exactly which stars to reach for.
They've built their rocket ship to outer space long ago,
and can navigate it to their destination with expertise.

But you?
You're stuck on earth,
your dreams too fanciful for what you can handle.
You want everything too much. You want nothing at all.

Fanciful: over-imaginative and unrealistic.
It's what they tell you your dreams are,
made out of dust and ready to be swept away.
Was there ever a lesson in school, however,
that required dreams to be still?

I am not a static being.
I am unsure; I am fanciful.
I am not an inherent flaw because of this.
Tell me I'm unrealistic; tell me I'm invalid.
But words don't extinguish flames.

AFNAN NAEEM

SUNLIGHT AND A POET

The rays of late sunlight spill
a haze of yellow
upon the lush tips
of untrodden grass.

As the dismal colours
of the evening start to
take over the land,
a worn-out poet sits
in hopes of stitching together
the right words.

A poet,
her words,
an omelet
in her mind.

Memories,
life's worries,
wondering
where home is.

JESSICA FENG

PAINT IT GREY

RACHEL RUMAS

ESCAPE

In the island in the clouds, she wanders. Alone in their world and perfectly alone in hers, she claps her hands; she yells. She runs through the trees and laughs at everything and nothing. She dances.

It's quiet, like sunrise. The quiet made for reverie. The wind rides the tranquil sea, whispering softly as it glides along the surface of the tide. Stay, please stay.

Gentle waves of white, whipped like foam, lap at the celestial coast. She breathes in tandem. Out and in. Ebb and flow.

She stays to be content and to atone. There is a reproach in her heart. A guilt, a reminder of forgetting. The flowing breeze, the land, they are happy. Happy, at least now that she is here.

The island, floating in the refuge of the sky, shudders and cracks with her every leave. Too long and it falters, falls. Too long and she forgets. And so she is sorry, she says. She cannot remember how long it has been. In each of her waking moments she wishes she were not. She wishes to escape. She wishes to be with her love, in paradise. Fantastical, like the stories. Better. This she knows. A promise to herself. This will be better.

And so after all this time, she returns.

For how long? The island is the first to ask. For how long this time? For how long may we be happy?

She presses her hands into the lush green. Heart heavy with a familiar sorrow, and an unfamiliar release, she answers. Tears in her eyes, threatening to fall. Forever.

SROBONA PODDER

THE FOUNTAIN FIGURE

A life in velvet was all I'd ever known: never having to want because everything was given to me before I could, and never knowing what it felt like to dream for something more. It's hard to imagine a time where that was ever the case, but memories serve in more than one way.

Check-In: It had been a long, exhausting journey from home to the welcome luxury of the hotel. Father was in a mood, like always, and little Clare was fast asleep in my lap. Father never even looked at her. He just felt, in some way, obligated to her, seeing as Clare's mother was some unfortunate mistress in one of the small villages he frequented. Nevertheless, she quickly became like a sister to me, and I never once resented her. The moment we stepped out of the car, it was no surprise that Father began ordering the hotel employees around like pack mules. I quickly gathered Clare's and my things and headed for the grand staircase, but out of the corner of my eye, I noticed that one of the bellhops was simply standing in the middle of the fountain, getting soaked to the skin. I wondered if that was another one of Father's ridiculous commands, but he was nowhere near the fountain. Too tired to make any further investigation, I took Clare to our suite.

Dinner: It was a banquet like none I had ever experienced. All servers were perfectly red and black down to the jacket buttons inscribed with the hotel insignia. Clare and I wove through the crowd to find my father waiting at the head of the largest table in the room. I apologized for being late before he could comment and quickly sat down with Clare. She immediately went for the spoon as any four-year-old would, but a stern look from me told her all she needed to know: one wrong move and Father would have it in for us for the rest of the trip. We were both to be on our best behaviour to impress his potential business partner. Bored of all the official talk, I began studying the dining hall. I was always observant of my surroundings and even more so of the things that seemed out of place; I seemed to connect to those things most of all. It wasn't long before I noticed the man from the fountain, except this time he was staring just as intently at me as I was at him. I quickly looked away, but regretted it once I did. Why should I look away? I had done nothing wrong. I looked back to see him still staring at me. I held his gaze until he slipped out one of the doors marked "Employees Only."

The Meeting: Luckily, I managed to slip away from the dinner early with Clare, and she fell fast asleep upon getting in bed. I took the opportunity to slip out to the balcony and take in the view of the courtyard. There was a slight breeze in the otherwise still environment, and despite the raging party in the dining hall, there was nothing more than the quiet buzz of a summer night. I noticed someone standing in the middle of the fountain, and was hardly surprised to see that it was the same man from before. This time I simply had had enough, so I checked to make sure Clare was asleep and made my way out to the courtyard. I must have been mad or something because this man was a complete stranger. He smiled when he saw me approaching. Hesitantly, I sat on the edge of the fountain, never letting him out of my sight.

"You were watching me earlier." He spoke before I had the chance to.

"Only because you were watching me," I retorted.

I waited for some clever comeback, but there was none. He simply smiled and apologized for the misunderstanding. I asked him what he was doing in the fountain, and to this day, I still do not quite have the answer. All I know is that the story he told after was what kept me there hours more than I had intended. He was a vagabond, travelling from village to village, seeking shelter where he could for the night, and picking up jobs along the way. He never once stayed in a place for longer than a week. Something about his lifestyle intrigued me, and I found myself yearning for everything he had: adventure and independence. What he asked me at the end of the night, however, proved to me that I never could have those things.

Farewell: I watched the mysterious man from my balcony the next morning as he walked off with a small bag of food and a clean shirt. He told me it was all he needed, and I couldn't have agreed more. Father had a fit when I walked in late the previous night, but a quick kiss on the cheek melted any tension between us. This was my life, and for the next few years, at least, he would look after me. Maybe someday I would take Clare and find a place of my own, but at the time, I had to accept this as my adventure.

I am still unsure of what I should or should not have done. I said no to the man because I could never have left Clare. She means the world to me, and I am sure that someday, we will find our own paths to travel and explore. At the same time, I can't help but wonder if my life would have been better off had I gone with the man. I remember one thing that the man said: "Dreams do not define us, but the choices we make, whether to follow those dreams or not, do." I can say one thing for sure now: I finally have a dream.

JOHN LOUISSE FERNANDEZ

BEAST

This pounding thought stuck in the darkest galaxies of my mind,
Like a beast that calls out for freedom,
Induces the desperation, fear, and hope for what could be.
This pounding thought stuck in the deepest, darkest galaxies of my mind,
That I do not know whether to love or to hate,
Induces the shame, guilt, and remorse for the past.

So I released the beast out of its bounds
Into the field of the unknown and the uncertainties.
With reluctance, I tore apart the walls;
I opened my galaxies and poured its contents into the world,
Vulnerable as a babe fresh out of the bloody womb,
Vulnerable as a bare soldier out in the battlefield,

Then regret dawned on me.

The pounding thought that was once stuck in the darkest galaxies of my mind
Called out for confinement, away from the pain of the open,
Like the beast unshackled from its custody.
Now, the pounding thought that was once stuck in the darkest galaxies of my mind,
Mourned for the known and the cage
Like the beast that used to call out for freedom.

QURAT DAR

GOLDEN BUTTERFLIES

Golden butterflies
Slipping through my fingers
Wings of whims and nonsense things
And happily-ever-afters
They flutter and weave and suddenly leave
Turning to sand in a storm
But of the surreal fleet, no simple feat,
I have stolen from the swarm
My prisoner lives beside my heart, hemmed in by ruthless bone,
Tattered, frenzied, and alone
I feed it thoughts, it pays my fee,
An unlikely, fragile detainee –
For I am man
And it, a dream.

NATHAN DUONG

PIANO

CHINMAYEE GIDWANI

CARPE DIEM

He walked along the road, kicking pebbles in his path. His life was a mess. His family had disowned him, the love of his life had walked out on him on their wedding day, and he had lost his job.

The cold wind chilled him to the bone on this fateful October night. The moon was out and casting a slight shadow on everything. Looking up, he tried to locate some constellations, but he couldn't see any. Whether this was due to his drunken state or light pollution in the city, he did not know.

On and on he walked, and he lost all sense of time and direction. It could've been days, and he could be on the other side of the country, and he wouldn't have known. He eventually walked onto a large bridge. *It's beautiful,* he thought.

He walked to the middle of the bridge, deciding he couldn't continue his journey any longer. He had lost everything, and he couldn't find the strength, physically or emotionally, to go on.

He cast his gaze upon the waves that would soon carry his body. They overlapped and grazed against the rocks ferociously, creating white foam. It was mesmerizing, just like everything else about this night.

He climbed over the ledge and leaned forward, kept on the bridge only by his arms. *This is it,* he thought. *My last act of cowardice.*

He closed his eyes as he let go of the bridge, ready to face his death.

"What do you think you're doing?" she yelled against the wind, pulling him back onto the ledge.

"I'm trying to die!" he screamed back.

"You can't do that!"

"Why not?!"

"Because I was here first, therefore, I reserve the right to jump off first!"

“That was cruel of you, bringing me back to this mad world,”

“It was cruel of you to leave me here, watching you escape the madness.”

He looked at her for the first time. She had soft, blond hair and startling green eyes that held passion. Being as bundled up as she was, it was difficult to discern any other features.

“We need to hurry up, someone might drive by and see us!” he said frantically.

“Shall we jump at the same time?” she replied, getting ready.

“No, that won’t do! I’ll go first. If there are any unexpected surprises in the afterworld, I can come back and warn you.”

“Anything is better than this vain world! Nonetheless, I was here first. *I’ll* go first and warn you if necessary,” she argued.

“Absolutely not! I’d hate to change my mind and return to the hell that is my life,” he said.

“Well, what do you propose we do?” she yelled, the wind getting stronger.

“I do believe th–” He was cut off by her scream, as she lost her balance.

He instinctively grabbed her arm and held onto the railing of the bridge with the other. She pulled herself up before turning to help him. They both lay down on the hard pavement of the sidewalk, catching their breaths.

“Well that was quite the adventure,” she remarked.

“Indeed,” he replied. “What is a pretty woman like you doing on a bridge at night, all alone?”

“The same thing a handsome young man like you is doing.” She smiled although it didn’t quite reach her eyes.

“Fair enough,” he laughed. “So, what made you want to jump?”

“I’d rather not discuss that,” she mumbled, looking away. “After all, it is what I hope to escape by jumping."

"No, I meant why did you *jump?"* She looked at him with confusion. "You could have stabbed yourself, or shot yourself. Hell, arsenic and cyanide aren't that hard to come by either!"

"Oh," her eyes widened in realization. "Well, I don't know."

"Then you can't jump. Not without knowing why you chose to jump, with a plethora of other methods available to you," he paused.

"Okay, I won't jump," she replied. "On one condition."

"Oh?" He raised his eyebrow.

"I want you to live as well," she said, sitting up.

"But that defeats the purpose of my proposal!" he exclaimed.

"It doesn't matter. If you go off that bridge, I will follow you," she pouted stubbornly. "Deal, or no deal?"

He smiled, a real and genuine smile, for the first time that night. He cupped her beautiful face in his large hands and looked her straight in the eyes.

"Deal."

"Alright," she laughed softly. Gesturing in one direction, she added, "Hey, let's go this way. I came from the other way, and it will be a physical and symbolic bridge I will have crossed."

"But I came from that way. I want to cross this symbolic bridge too!" he exclaimed.

"Of course," she sighed. "Okay, how about you go that way, and I'll go this way. I'll meet you downtown."

"Where in downtown?" he asked.

"Fate brought us on the same bridge last night, and if it's meant to be, it will bring us together again."

She started walking off the bridge, and he had no choice but to begin his trek in the other direction, and have faith in fate.

He chuckled to himself. How ironic; the only way to save her life was to save his own.

He felt joyous, rejuvenated, like a phoenix born out of the ashes. Nothing much had changed; he was still alone and abandoned. No, he was not alone anymore. Deep down, he knew he would find her again. Maybe not today, or tomorrow, but some day he would.

Walking off the Golden Gate Bridge early in the morning, with a killer hangover and old, oversized clothes, he found himself shedding his regrets. After all, every mistake leads to another opportunity. He discovered that the past must be remembered, respected, and used to march towards the future with stagnant tenacity.

And perhaps he also learned most important of all lessons to be learned in one's life: he had learned to seize the day.

NASHWA KHAN

HOMELANDLESSNESS

Laila felt displaced since childhood. There was no belonging anywhere; homelandlessness was omnipresent. Her desire for belonging ate at her and left her starving for acceptance. Embarking on this journey, she felt she would continue feeling hollow. She was abroad for the first time, travelling to the place her mother called "home." Her mother had crossed an ocean over 22 years ago to labour in the American dream, breaking a sea of sapphires in half for a country that didn't want her.

In a cab from the airport to the home her mother always told her she had; to the home her mom always emphasized as theirs, although Laila had never seen it. Broken Darija left her lips, letting the taxi driver know that Situ's house was in Ayn Diab in Casablanca.

Glancing out the window, there was a beach speckled with people laughing and smiling; it looked welcoming. These people were acquaintances to her ears, but strangers in her eyes. Waves receded like arms opening for a long-needed hug. Laughter could be heard; it cut through the traffic like sun breaking through storm clouds.

Rays of sunlight danced through the window in slivers as the taxi passed carts with vendors selling the succulent summer fruit she had only heard about from her mother. Cactus and citrus, vibrant in hues and bright like stars, stood out on the landscape of the carts. The morning tasted bitter; her tongue lingered with unrequited love.

Laila could not reciprocate the embrace of the shore; the disappearing waves continued to beckon like an adult to a waddling toddler. Walking up the stairs, the smell of couscous wafted thickly like a brick wall; this place smelt peculiarly of home. Uneasy, she led herself up the worn and crooked stairs, grazing the cool geometrical tile with the tips of her fingers. Her heart began to skip, not in the ways it skipped when she interacted with a boy she liked, but an anxious skip. Her muscles started to freeze up like a bucket filled with ice had been dumped on her.

Like an old wooden bridge with the weight of a dozen trucks, she felt herself splintering, slowly splitting apart and succumbing to the weight of finally being in this place that her mama called "home." Her olive face became as pale as the moon, the weight of a thousand bricks hitting her as she realized that this was her last chance at finding "home."

The "Beckies" and "Tinas" that filled her North American classrooms didn't need to find "home." They had theirs. Their names didn't twist tongues and faces like hers did. Though she resisted being othered, she didn't quite fit in, with her complexion that made peers uncomfortable and her mama who didn't look like theirs.

The stairs, like a labyrinth in a never-ending corn maze, continued; her hand got heavy against the tiles blanketing the walls. The tiles encased the walls like a shell encasing the inhabitants.

Situ singing the Rai music her mama loved floated through a jarred large wooden door, and as she went to open the door, she felt her heart ease, the weight of the bricks gone. As her Situ turned, face warm, smelling of flower water and arms open like the shore, she saw a face like hers; this was home. The sun poured through the windows and embraced them both as her tears fell down like drops down a window; she belonged. Laila knew now that she had been oceans away from her soul, and was now whole.

Glossary
Darija: Moroccan Arabic
Situ: Grandma
Couscous: Traditional Maghrebian dish of semolina, cooked by steaming

LUCIA SALVATI

REGAINING STRENGTH THROUGH PEACE AND TRANQUILITY

PETRA KIM

THE DREAM CATCHER

Restless, he stirs under the shadow of dusk,
Gaze straying to the remnants of the bygone dust
Once there, painting the sky in a palette of hue;
Its painter, now gone, has bid it adieu.

Has Raven forgotten to remove her ebony feathers;
Does she wish to keep the fragments of his stardust treasures?
Gingerly, fingers trembling like wind against the stillborn leaf,
Gathering the dull twinkle of Erstwhile's belief.

A Catcher he is,
Savouring wistful shades of Forlorn Painter's ashes,
And though he mourns, ragged breaths as a plea,
A Receiver he shall never be.

The harsh savour of the painter's wistful desires

For he is but the Catcher,
Wanting nonetheless to be the Receiver

Shades of wistfulness,
Mourning for he knows no further

In wistfulness mourns he, for he knows no further
Than the melancholy of the forsaken observer

For he is but the Catcher,
Wanting nonetheless to be the Receiver

HANNAH LUO

GONE FOREVER

KELLY ESTOMO

THIS BETTER BE MY LAST SONG ABOUT YOU

I've looked you in the face countless times with my
head guarded under elbows and
eyes like locked doors.

I don't see you at all when I'm awake.

There's a deep bass line that could
rumble from underneath the earth's crust and
shatter everything we know
in front of us,

only if we hit the right note.

Tonight,
the bass drum will be my racing pulse,
and our riffs will ride my lifeline like
an endless succession of tidal waves.

Tonight, I'll forget to dream about you.

Because our bones could only dream of the spinal chords we'll strum,
and the
blood in my head is a compressed soda can,
and I will soon,
surely,
forget about you,

because everything I plead for in melodic tongue is my naked soul, it's
everything I stand for in real time,
and it's not for you anymore.

So tonight, I promise to sleep with
our songs as my soundtrack
without your name in it.

RENA GAO

THE DINNER TABLE IS SILENT

The dinner table is silent.
I sit and my mind whorls to a thousand million places,
And the dinner table is silent.

The clink of spoons and the smacking of mouths
Echo around the dining room,
And the dinner table is silent.

The bright lights
Blind my soul
As the dinner table is silent.

Glitter of the lights, it reflects off the glasses
Of my juice, and pierces my heart;
The dinner table is silent.

My mind wanders to everywhere and nowhere
Let bygones be bygones, they tell me
The dinner table is silent.

There's too much silence, it confuses the mind
The soul craves for a bowl of hot soup
The dinner table is silent.

Wishful thinking,
Hungry for more,
The dinner table is silent.

Let my soul wander
And escape this predicament
As the dinner table is silent.

The seasons change
And day turns to night, yet

The dinner table is silent.

The faces of the familiar swim into vision,
And I open my mouth to speak
As the dinner table is silent.

The dinner table is silent.
The wind howls on outside the window, the cat crawls underneath the window ledge,
The moon shines on in a blaze of glory, and I speak.

"Pass the salt, please."

PETRA KIM

MIRAGE

RACHEL TRAN

WHITE MATTER

He was wandering in the cold night, his warm breath making wisps of smoke in the frigid air. The moon was full, cascading ethereal beams of light onto the forest. The demented shadows cast by the naked trees poured onto the white, untouched snow. So perfect was it amid the cacophony created by the wind, and now his footsteps were to ruin its beauty. The marks of his worn boots trailed the forest every time it snowed. He could not stand the placid white matter that fell from the sky. He envied it. His entire life had been a failure, and he seemed to think the snow was gloating at him, silently snickering at his feeble attempts to achieve what he had wanted to achieve.

He began to stomp at the newly fallen snow, each step representing a dream he had dreamed and had tried to accomplish but never did. Why could he not do it? What stood between him and success? *Nothing,* he thought. *Just the snow and* her. She was the one who had encouraged him to continue his endeavours, to dream, to hope. What had been meant to be positive support had turned into lies and disappointment.

"You can do it," she had always said. "You are special. Dream big. How do you know you can't do it? You'll never know until you try. And even when you fail, you always get back up on your feet and try again."

Try again. He scoffed. "The harder you try, the harder you fall," he mumbled to the bone-chilling howls of the wind. The ground was now dotted with one hundred fifty footsteps; he had counted. One hundred fifty dreams, infinite failures.

He could have continued to walk. He should have—he had many more dreams to recall—but something stopped him, an unknown force. He stood still, wanting to walk, yet knowing that he would regret the action. Something was growing inside his heart, something warm and invigorating. It began as the tiny glow of a single light, the light one saw at the end of an abyss that was said to have never ended. It was a spark of hope, and more and more of his heart was lit up with it. He had not felt this way in a very long time, this remnant of satisfaction and joy. He stood straighter and rolled his shoulders. The muscles around his mouth started to contort in manner he thought they had forgotten. The invisible lump on his back that had always weighed tonnes now rivaled the weight of snowflakes that escaped the sky.

This was how he felt when he had first seen her, in all her radiance.

This was how he felt when she had first saved him.

When she had told him to restart and be resilient for the first time, he had truly believed that things would get better. He had truly believed in his own capabilities. With her beside him, he could knock down the tallest brick wall, climb the highest mountain, swim across the widest ocean.

Just as suddenly as the feeling came, the warmth fled from his heart, leaving a gaping hole of longing that could never be closed. If he accomplished all of his dreams, it still would have never completely filled that part of his soul that had been ripped away many years ago. He had made her leave, for her own good, and at the time he felt proud of hurting her. If she had stayed with him, they would have both suffered, and he would have never lived with himself.

Underneath his mask of pride, he had been in agony. He still was now, wandering in the forest on this exceptionally cold and frigid night.

He continued to walk again, and erased all thoughts of her with his meticulous counting. *One hundred fifty-one, one hundred fifty-two, one hundred fifty-three...*

HANNAH LUO

JAMAIS-VU

ALINE-CLAIRE HUYNH

AND SHE WORE MOONLIGHT

And she wore moonlight on her skin, fresh snow and air swirling 'round like the first fallings, lips that ghosted what was once beautiful, once lovely, once loving. Oh – how the steps she took were alive, fast fleeting pitter-patters across the wind-swept plains of frozen grass, billowing gently in Nyx's domain. Her very self, curved like the scythe of death's embrace coming swift. The bow of her body tilted and arched, taut like the strongest of strings being pulled for an arrow, an aim, a target.

As the twang sent her back up, her mark hit strong and true, and there bloomed the first crimsons on the whites of his once smooth plains, inevitably interrupted with the flourishing water of life and the pommel of Death herself sprouting delicately from the fountain. A gasp, the last murmurs of great power in ruins, and a painting of a smile blossomed as she drank the last words to be spoken and kept them only to herself. The last righteous seal on the doors of breath, warmth still emanating from its silken curves, and all was still as time froze, cold like her beauty. With a departing last farewell, adieu and not au revoir, she let go of a love once lost then found, and he tilted over like a wooden doll, nothing but a figurine off-balance, gracefully letting the air surround his body going down, down, down, like the new snow from the skies.

Artemis from above shone down, and with her the Hunt was over, collapsing in herself as the first droplets fell from the windows of her soul, the smile fallen like a broken bird dragged down by the pure white weights.

RYAN CHU

ERROR

Grey clouds are creeping across the sky
over rain-slickened roads
clogged with burnt cigarettes.

The world slows down,
stagnation settles like a fog,
epitaphs crumble to dust.

I am trapped in this clockwork prison,
this photograph blurred at the edges,
this suffocating world of monochrome.

I peer through the window and see the pale faces,
umbrellas, trenchcoats making their way through the flooded city.

I can hear the blood running through my veins,
one pulse after another after another,
perfectly synced with the rhythmic tick-tock
that echoes through empty space.

.

.

.

Sometimes I wonder what it would be like
if this silent world of monochrome
discovered even a single
fragment of
colour.

Dao Mun Lim

The Jumpshot

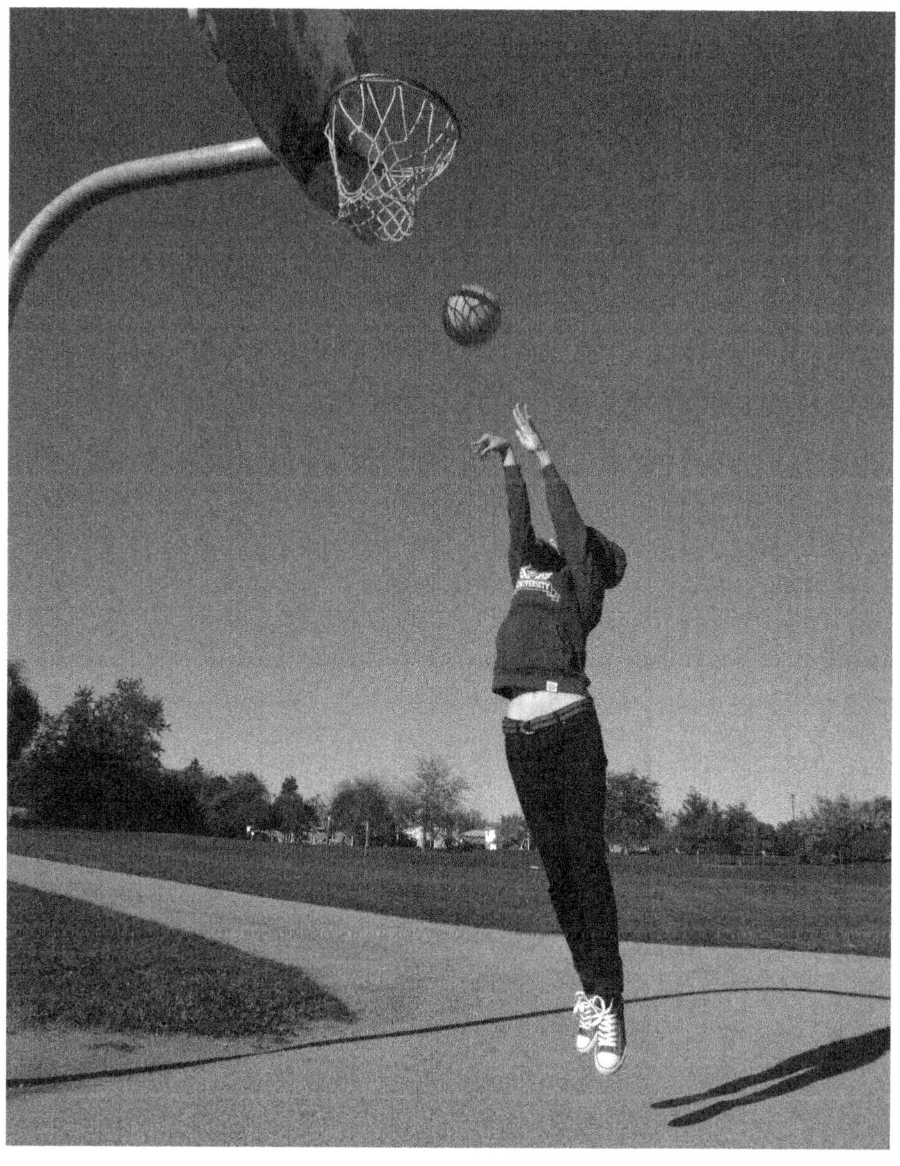

FATHAMA ARSHAD

HOW I AM NOW

Ironic how the sky depicts my mood. I hate the rain. Hate it. Not only does it make the sky look dull and sad and leave the streets empty of people, it leaves me feeling dull and sad and empty as well. And when I am feeling those things and the rain is sobbing on the streets, I think of you and your devil smile. I think of you and your eyes that swim in a thousand different colours. I think of you and your hands that were softer than mine and how I hated you for that. I hate you now for everything else too. If you could see my heart, you'd see scars and bruises and cuts and wounds, and you'd see how ugly it's become. You'd see how it beats infrequently, and you'd see how it's hanging on by a thread. Remember when you jokingly said you were stealing the colour from my eyes to add more to yours? It scares me because that's exactly what you did. You stole my ability to love as well. And when the moon comes up at night, I shut my blinds and pull the covers over my face because you told me you loved the way the moon lights up the room and reminds you that I'm always here. I realize now that you were not afraid of losing me, you were afraid of the dark. And whenever I go to the beach I roll up my jeans and stand ankle deep in the water because you hated to do that so I never did it, and now I do this everyday. I buy all the junk food I can buy because you said, "ladies shouldn't binge,"; now I wish you were here to watch me eat. I used to love counting stars until you came along and you told me it was weird and a waste of time because I would never be able to count all of them. Now I count stars like my life depends on it. You creep into every little thing that I do, and I do all these things to get rid of every little piece of you. My heart thrashes in my chest, and it's as if there's a tsunami in my throat, and it's all because of you. I remind myself everyday that if you were to see me in seven years' time, everything about me will be different. I will have completely new blood cells running through my body, my eyes will be the colour of me, and my heart will be healed. My skin will be one that you've never touched, and if you happen to recognize me, I hope you don't say hi.

IBRAHIM ISSA

LANDING

INAARA PANJWANI

THE POEM TREE

Yesterday in class, my teacher read me *poemtry*
The words made me happy; they formed pictures for me to see
I reached out to catch them, like apples falling from a tree

A tree of passion, hopes, dreams, and thoughts,
Growing from deep beneath the ground
Its words bloomed as flowers, and its fruit was ripe with passion
Ideas branched from its trunk and reached out to me
The tree was a poem tree

I built a fort from its leaves
And climbed its branches to highest of heights
I lay down as its roots wrapped around me
Its shade sheltered me from sunlight

Today I'll go back to this tree of mine
And carve some words of my own
Into its trunk, and make it my home

CINDY LIN

DOOM

In the freezing arms of the night,
our impending doom may seem inevitable,
but remember that magic exists in crooks and crannies,
places you no longer remember to look.

JASJEET DHALIWAL

12 AM IN A FOREIGN CITY

12 am in a foreign city. It could have been Paris; it could have been New York; I cannot recall. All I can remember from that night is the light breeze that drifted past me and sitting on the balcony enjoying a smoke, deep within my thoughts. Not chilly, the kind of breeze that is easy to enjoy. Music flew in with the breeze – jazzy, the type that reminds you of days past. I took to seclusion like someone who is forced to repeatedly do that which he or she does not enjoy. At the beginning, you are filled with despair; however, as it is with many other things, the less you struggle, the easier you drift into the void. And there, you sit perched upon the mountain, living a constant bird's eye view.

As I sat there on the hotel balcony, I sifted through memories sparked by the jazz. It felt like a lifetime ago, but just a couple years ago, I was on the "right" path. A path to glory, a path to actually becoming someone. I spent my childhood and adolescent years dreaming. I dreamt of a better tomorrow and forgot my bitter yesterdays. I dreamt of achievement. It was refreshing thinking away my sorrows, like falling asleep after a bad day, except on a much grander scale. Like most creative adolescents, my mind could never focus entirely on one thing.

Before, I was quietly rising up the corporate ladder, sitting safe and secure while engrossed in my highly repetitive and unsatisfying lifestyle. Now, I feel both free and enlightened. Before, I constantly asked myself: How can the masses be so easily subdued and stripped of their passions like sheep? We flock together behind shepherds and conform under their leadership. I saw no sense in this, so I quit my job, a move highly questioned by my friends and family. They never understood my motives. Did it surprise me? I can't say it did. They never have understood.

I now spend my days walking the rich streets of my hometown, soaking in all the colour. Sometimes I feel like I soak in too much, for the more I learn, the more dull the world seems to me. I was never captivated by the joys and wonder of life. I spend my days entirely underwhelmed. When I'm filled to the brim with colour, I pick up the brush that is my pencil, and I spray upon the canvas that is this page.

Phases, moods, feelings, sentiments. My thoughts are heavily cluttered; my mind foggy. My mind bleeds more than my veins yet less than my heart. I've been through much, yet I realize much more is in store. I've taken up a job at a local corner store. It helps me to stay sane and pay my way. I hope these thoughts and this effort are not in vain. *They are my torch, my way out of the darkness*, I think, as I drift into a deep sleep. My life is chaos, but in this moment I feel a powerful peace. I drift into nothingness and turn into the dirt I was once raised from. This period of nightly reflection has become a routine.

12 AM in a foreign city. It could have been Paris; it could have been New York.

VAIBHAV YADARAM

CHILDHOOD ESSENTIALS

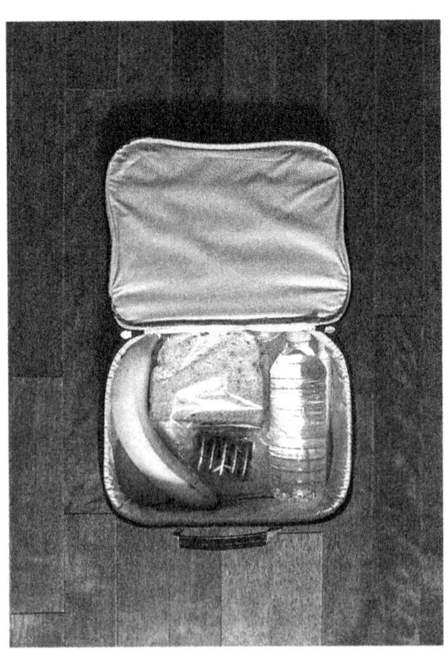

CHELSEA TAO

ROOM #3

Cluttered, the old desk sorts itself against plywood;
in its corner, red dusted trails and a tiny handprint
marks the room with patience.
Tacked into the audience of off-coloured peach drywall
are directions to Purgatory, Burning Man, Vienna,
infused with Swahili battle breath
or breathlessly named under British sun once,
everywhere now resting on its bones,
watching the world spin gold from its expired years.
Like a decade old joke,
the clock chuckles at the memory, not the ransom
of humour now tied behind its back;
the idea is to laugh it off whenever the hours are cheated.
It knows the pull of midnight smoke; this mirror
is as unchanging as the denial of free flight.
Between its hands are dozens of unspoken prayers,
hard-pressed as if tempted to find their way back
to a time when they were not needed.
In its eyes, reflection is a vise on potency,
lasting as long as the mind pays judgment,
overcome by the flaw of humanity,
saved by the familiarity of disappointment.

HAJER MUSTAFA

PAW-NDERING

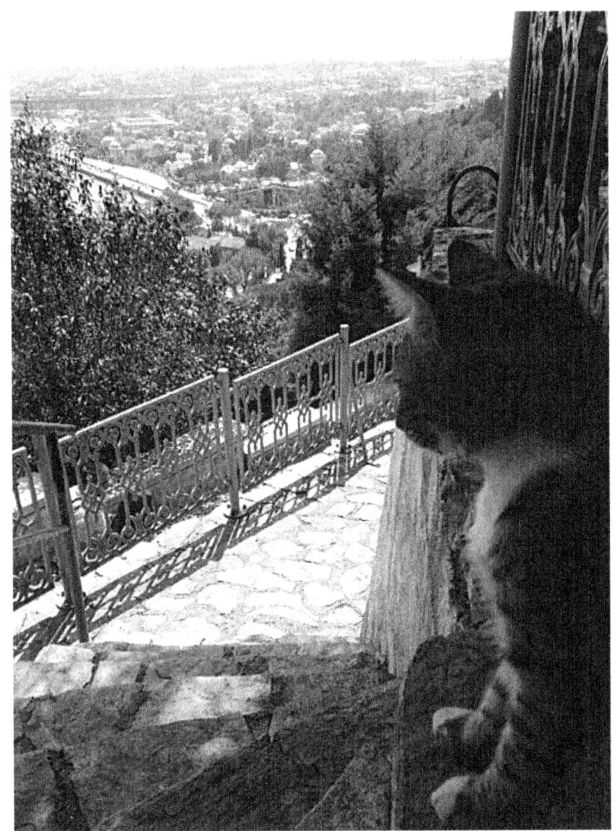

EMILY CUMMINGS

DEMEYES

The light coming in from the window lived in his eyes, brightening their color; making them luminescent. The unremarkable hazel coming alive. The color of spring, the color of miles and miles of forest stretching out forever. Endless. The color of a glittering peridot, of joy and laughter for that's what it seemed like the light was doing in them. Glistening, dancing; they changed me. In that moment I felt my heart stir. It was like I hadn't known my favourite color until I saw him. His face however gave nothing away; calmly he stared into the yard, his strong arms resting on the tabletop. Around us, people were talking. Maybe to me, perhaps to him but if they were he gave no indication. I couldn't hear anything distinctive either, all I could see were his eyes. It seems a bit weird looking back, how completely mesmerized I was. What he must have thought of me, just staring at him. As unfriendly as his face looked, I trusted him. I trusted those eyes because they told a different story than the impassive mask. They told me that they were happy, that they knew love and friendship, that they were kind. They beckoned to me, showed me beauty, showed me soul. Like a good book or a gorgeous sunset, I just couldn't look away. I wanted to know more about those eyes. What did they look like when he laughed? When he cried? The whole world was gone, everything moving in slow motion except for the light glowing in his deep pools of kaleidoscopic sensation. And then they moved and I went into cardiac arrest. Not truly, though that would make for a great first impression. His eyes shifted to mine, the brilliant gems meeting my dull irises. And just as quickly they shifted away, dismissive, bored. The eyes didn't glow when they searched mine, they didn't vibrate with life like they had just a moment ago. And he never looked back.

Gena Zheng

My Childhood Home

fresh spices fill the air
rosemary and thyme graze the noses of children
sizzling meat on the pan crackle alongside the whistling kettle
the friendliness of fire accompanied by
the dolls and plush toys coming to life
each character assumed a role; a name, a personality, an action
today, it was a bank heist: Peter the Panda was the robber
Katie the Kitten was an undercover secret agent
Peter almost got away, as he screamed, “you'll never take me alive”
Katie answered, “not on my watch”
and the outbursts continued, intertwined with giggles and
determination from their puppet masters
purposefully positioned in proper placement

playing will resume momentarily
everybody is here
except mommy and daddy
but that's the usual
and their presence is not missed

the table covered with many little side dishes
the green of the vegetables mixed with the tiny grains of rice
the kids devour their entrées
so they can find out what happens to Peter and Katie

MINHA MOHSIN

PERSPECTIVE

NASHWA KHAN

PIZZA DAY

Nashwa looked in the mirror, her heart sinking as she saw that her face had not changed since the last time she had grimaced at her reflection. She ran her hands over her wiry hair and twisted her face. She often avoided the large, mirrored walls of the school bathroom as a form of self-care. The more she avoided the mirror, the more she could envision herself as lighter with features more like her peers. Nashwa was disrupted suddenly when she heard the obnoxious call of the lunch bell. She dragged herself out of the washroom, her feet weighed down by invisible cement blocks. She hoped her mother was here today.

It was Pizza Day, another day in which she would unnecessarily justify to her peers that she always chose cheese or vegetarian because of animal rights and not because of her Islamic faith. Kids with religious dietary restrictions went first; vegetarians who avoided meat for animal rights waited. The other children were seated at long plastic tables like rows of eggs. They would scowl bitterly as the warm, savoury scent of pizza wafted through the cafeteria. Fuming, the other children would whine at this true injustice, thinking of the "reverse racism" in those moments. Pizza Day would be a small weekly battle, iterations of it being rehashed throughout university, a battlefield going beyond the cafeteria's white cinder block walls and cloudy linoleum floors.

After September 11, 2001, things became tougher for kids like Nashwa. Before, the cinnamon coloured Muslim kids could blend in with the Hispanic kids or be accepted by the black kids; however, after 9/11, the few Muslim kids at Windermere Elementary were pariahs to everyone in rural Florida. Nashwa didn't blame old friends who turned into foes; they were just trying to survive, navigating the sea of whiteness they were drowning in.

Trying to avoid any markers of otherness, Nashwa worked hard to keep her Muslim identity on the down-low. She made sure that she mimed the popular white girls, saved lunch money to buy the right clothes, and attempted to flatten her curly hair until it began to present symptoms of heat damage. Her hair reminiscent of a scarecrow's, Nashwa traded her flat iron for daily hairspray to tame the straggly baby hairs predominant on children of colour.

She was relieved that her mother did not wear a hijab and could pass as white. Nashwa would worry about her mother's slight accent, but this was trumped by her mother's porcelain exterior. Bringing her to school events felt like showing off a report card with a 4.0 average; her mother's blue eyes and pale skin were a security blanket. In those moments when people would elate, "Your mother is white?! Her eyes are blue?! She's so beautiful," Nashwa would gleefully reply, unfolding herself slowly, correcting her posture to a confident stance, smoothing down her wiry hair, "Yes, that's my mom! I know her features are beautiful!" She would savour the words, extending the moments with fillers like "I'm just tanned because I swim a lot." Nashwa would find ways to approximate herself to this coveted whiteness her mother and peers had. She would prolong her brief tango with whiteness, beckoning her mother over to introduce to people. She saw her mother encompassed in an aureole of whiteness as she floated gracefully towards her.

Nashwa would Band-Aid the subtext of feeling inadequate with her mother's Eurocentric beauty, finding solace in the fact that people appreciated an extension of her in those moments. In those moments she would taste victory and her white mother was a trophy. When her mother volunteered with the white mothers on Pizza Day, Nashwa's chest would swell with pride like the gaudy inflatable decorations her classmates adorned their houses with every December.

Nashwa dragged her feet out of the cafeteria, weighed down again by cement blocks; more battles were to ensue in the classroom, and her mother would not be in the backdrop to relish and centralize.

CHELSEA TAO

JANUARY

January, a pale thing
barely distinguishable through the patchwork of a
confused all-creator. Mixed frenzy and a hatred
distinct with always
an eternity is carved from whoever's God is up there.
Still sitting and sitting still against an ancient second
held up by a trillion bonds, an elegy for the expired
rings into heaven or vendetta it screams in Terrarian tongue
I am your forever, I am everything you have lived for.
Give it a temporary, give it humanity
and now this God knows the price of having nothing.

NEHA CHOLLANGI

LOST MOMENTS

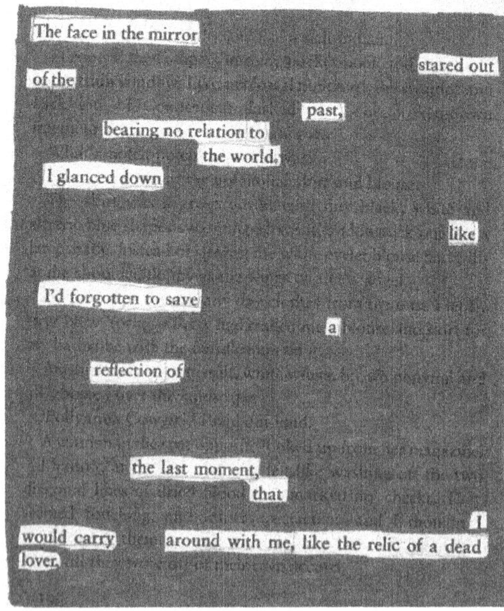

The face in the mirror
stared out
of the
past,
bearing no relation to
the world.
I glanced down
like
I'd forgotten to save
a
reflection of
the last moment,
that
I
would carry
around with me, like the relic of a dead
lover.

KRISTEN LORITZ

STEVE AND ALLEN

Blessed are the ectomorphs: the skinny mini's and naturally thigh-gapped women of the world – or so the marketing industry claims. *Toned bodies, we want toned bodies,* they say. New images of thinness promote strength, but still showcase slim ideals. Athletes *should* represent the pinnacle of fitness and desire, yet magazines like *Women's Health* slap these athletes with aesthetic failure. Slender ideals work against what many fitness gurus and athletes need in order to succeed, including the development of thick, strong, muscular – whatever you want to call them – thighs.

In *Making Sense of Muscle: The Body Experiences of Collegiate Women Athletes*, Molly George (2005)[1] says female athletes experience pressure when it comes to physical physique, and strive "to build just the right amount of 'sexy, feminine' muscle" (p. 317). The *right amount of sexy* apparently lies within the pages of newspapers, blogs, and magazines like *Women's Health*. With bold fonts, skinny legs, and *slim down* rhetoric, these articles tickle viewers sweet senses and prepare their taste buds to consume an appetizing combination of images and verbosity.

Picture your thirteen-year-old self gazing in the mirror. What do you see? Braces and pimples? I see *sausage legs*: thighs bigger than my peers, warranting an obsession with slimming them. Now look at the perfectly shaped, smooth, and thin legs of the *Woman's Health* models. Photoshop's delicate digital surgery appears to bless these babes with a thigh gap. *Los Angeles Times* writer, Mary McNamara (2014)[5] describes the gap and its allure:

> "A thigh gap, for the six people still unfamiliar with the term, is created by thighs so slender they do not touch when a woman stands with her feet together. One does not have to get all "Da Vinci Code" divine-feminine about it to argue that it has become the holy grail of female body obsession" (para 3).

The difficulty in attaining a thigh gap presents a challenge and challenges fuel athletes, and alas, a dangerous mix is born. We forget we do not *need* to look like the models; we forget why we *want* to look like models because we forget the media creates and perpetuates these models and their fictionalized standards.

⁘

A knife and fork clatters as Carla scrapes at the last morsel of chicken on her plate. The restaurant vibrates with chatter as my teammates inhale their dinner. Sam remains silent amongst the chaos. Across from Carla, I watch Sam lift her napkin and release it. The delicate white edges of the cloth droop and parachute down onto her steaming plate. The fabric drapes over her food the way a doctor would cover a cadaver. Sam twirls her fork and stares at her napkin. Her grey eyes hung heavy like lead balloons in their socket. Whispers of Sam's anorexia spread among the team.

Sam is fifteen.

⁘

At sixteen, my small figure represents an internal source of pride, allowing me to take on the role of team 'guinea pig.' Raised and tossed like a stringless puppet, my teammates lift and contort my small frame above the ice and above their heads. I never hit the ground. For the first time, my legs are the smallest of them all.

Then Steve and Allen entered my life; a subtle arrival that spanned several years of late nights at the rink, afternoons at the gym, and sunny weekends running outside along the Toronto lakeshore.

⁘

At eighteen, the rookie days of soaring above my teammates eventually ceased, thanks to Steve and Allen.

⁘

No longer would my petite-ness receive praise or attention, thanks to Steve and Allen.

⁘

Steve and Allen, so my teammates deem them, are my thighs.

Black spandex hugs twenty-three pairs of sore legs. I catch a glimpse of the full length mirror that runs along the short axis of the arena. The mirror reflects a tall slender figure dressed in black. A narrow crevasse separates her legs into two distinct cylinders. I squint.

Maria's head peeks out from the change room door. "Where the hell did Steve and Allen go?" Maria shouts. "My legs are bigger than yours now!"

Instead of fuming from Maria's words, instead of yearning for another round of squats, instead of crushing my competitive spirit, Maria awoke a voice inside me that said, *you are good enough now.*

Without the strength and endurance of Steve and Allen, I am nothing as an athlete. The fulfillment of a media constructed standard lead to the disintegration of a real standard: my fitness at the cost of sexy, feminine, and ideal. The less I ran, the skinnier my legs became, and the more I succumbed to the very forces that drove Sam into a mental, physical, and emotional disorder. *Was I on this path too?*

Shame set in. The shame of knowing I gave into an institutionalized fabrication, the shame of knowing I could not help my friend. In a few weeks, Steve and Allen would grow plump until the next training camp, and so the cyclical cycle continues; a waxing and waning of faux happiness and athletic dissatisfaction.

Women's Health needs to 'work out' their portrayal of women's bodies. But hold on! A recent search on their website shows positive signs of change, showcasing articles like Goldman's (2014) *There Are Now 'Anti-Thigh Gap' Jeans*[2] and Gueren's (2013) *More Proof That the "Thigh-Gap Trend" Is Ridiculous*[3]. But at the same time, the magazine still provides the latest tips and tricks on how to slim your thighs and features the same gapless models on their cover pages. Thanks for trying, *Women's Health.* To my fellow athletes and women: stop seeking these outlets as exemplary material and start looking at the people who surround you. Beauty encompasses a vast spectrum and is not a definable point on this continuum. Instead of indulging in a thigh gap, I say, forget that. Time to embrace Steve and Allen as a tool, a foundation and a source of strength, because I am not a showpiece.

And I'm okay with that.

NEHA CHOLLANGI

THE KNOBLESS DOOR

JULIVER RAMIREZ

NANAY

The metal flap of the mail slot flips open. My little sister's eyes squint through the hole in the front door. Elise surveys our grandma's small apartment.

Elise moves her mouth to the mail slot. She breathes in and calls out, "Naaaanaaaaay! Open the door!" Pops knocks on the door over Elise's yelling.

"*Hoy*, quieter," Mom whisper-yells at Pops. She gestures at the neighboring doors. I look down the second floor hallway. Silence.

Krisa, my older sister, looks up from her phone. "Can we just use the key already?" she begs Pops.

"No, *Kree-sa*, that's rude. It's only for emergencies," Mom butts in.

"But we *always* use it if she doesn't answer in like five minutes," Krisa fires back. "Come on, Papa. I still have a bio lab to do at home."

"Yeah, same boat. I have an American literature paper. Haven't started," I add.

Mom kisses her teeth and shoots us a stern look. Pops fishes his key ring out of his pocket and sifts through it for the spare key.

Nanay softly wheezes in her sleep. She lies as stiff as the coil-sprung bed she naps on.

Pops, Mom, Krisa, Elise, and I file into Nanay's cluttered room at the end of the narrow hallway. Two stacks of folded laundry lean against each other by the foot of her bed. Two big brown boxes destined for the Philippines—but never making the trip—serve as makeshift tables for her bags, medication bins, and old newspaper flyers. Her dresser-turned-altar takes up the most space in the room. On it, crucifixes, candles, and small statues of Mother Mary and Santo Niño de Cebú collect a film of dust.

Pops approaches Nanay and gives her shoulder a gentle shake. She doesn't move. Pops shakes a little harder. "'*Nay*, wake up," he says in his softest voice.

Nanay's eyes slowly open. She doesn't flinch. She doesn't yell out in surprise. She's the most graceful nap-taker in the world. She smiles at each of us and waves.

⁘

In the family room, my parents and sisters watch *Eat Bulaga*, a Filipino game show. My family's greetings—simple hi's, how are you's, did you eat lunch yet's, did you go to church today's—did not last long. I stay behind to help Nanay before joining everyone in the family room. Nanay sits on the side of her bed as I move around. I am an extension of her eyes, arms, and feet.

"Do you see my hair tie, *balong*?" Nanay asks. I like the way she calls me 'boy' in her Ilocano tongue. She always fills the word with endearment so it sounds like "my boy," as if she's telling me she's proud to have me.

"Here's one." I pick up a hair tie lying on one of the brown boxes and hand it to her.

As she holds the tie between her pursed lips, Nanay combs her fingers through the roots of her silver hair. She gathers it all in her left hand as if she's starting a ponytail. With her right, she takes the mass of hair and winds it around itself. She cinches the bundle into place with the tie. Nanay always wears her bun this way. I like the way she doesn't change it.

"My medicine, *balong*?"

I scan the heap for orange pill bottles. There are a lot. "Umm... which one?"

"Hah?" Nanay turns her ear towards me.

"Which. One." I shrug and make a couple confused expressions. "I. Don't. Know. Which. Medicine."

Behind her baggy eyes, my message takes a few seconds to process. Nanay waves me away and leans forward, shifting her body weight to stand up. I spring for her cane, place it under her hand, and help her up. Nanay takes one step forward, bends down, collects three bottles, turns, and eases herself back into her spot on the bed. I hand her the water bottle from her night table.

Nanay cups one of each pill in her palm and gulps them. The water in the bottle quivers with every tremor in her hand. She sits, letting her medication settle. Nanay looks around her mess of a room like a lost yet brave child in a shopping mall.

I sit on the floor by Nanay's feet. I hold her hand. I don't do things like this as often as I should, so she smiles at me, happy.

Her hand looks like a conch shell; her knuckles like little spires, her skin like coarse husk. From under it, faint green and purplish veins bulge. They fan out under the splatters of liver spots. But inside the shell, the palm I clasp now, the core is a smooth and warm place to find comfort.

My free hand traces and retraces the biggest veins. They don't stay down. I smile at her milky grey eyes.

Nanay's arthritis-warped hand squeezes back at mine. Her crooked thumb caresses my thumb. The motion is small. Strained.

I try to think about the things those hands have gone through. I try to think about how the years of labour in the Philippines twisted her body so that my family could be where we are today: Canada.

I can't imagine.

What did Nanay do for a living when she was young? I don't know. What did she want to do with her life? Did she end up doing it? I don't even know that. No one's ever told me. I don't think I ever asked.

I weigh these questions in my mind. As I fumble with the wording, more questions come to me. *Would she hear my questions properly? Would she understand me at all? She can barely understand Pops when he speaks to her in Ilocano.* I let the questions go.

I release her hand and pick myself off the floor. Her baby powder scent tickles my nose as I lean in to kiss her wrinkly jowls.

"I love you, Nanay."

"I love you too, *balong*."

That, she always understands.

ERICA YARMOL-MATUSIAK

MY INDUSTRIAL PARADISE

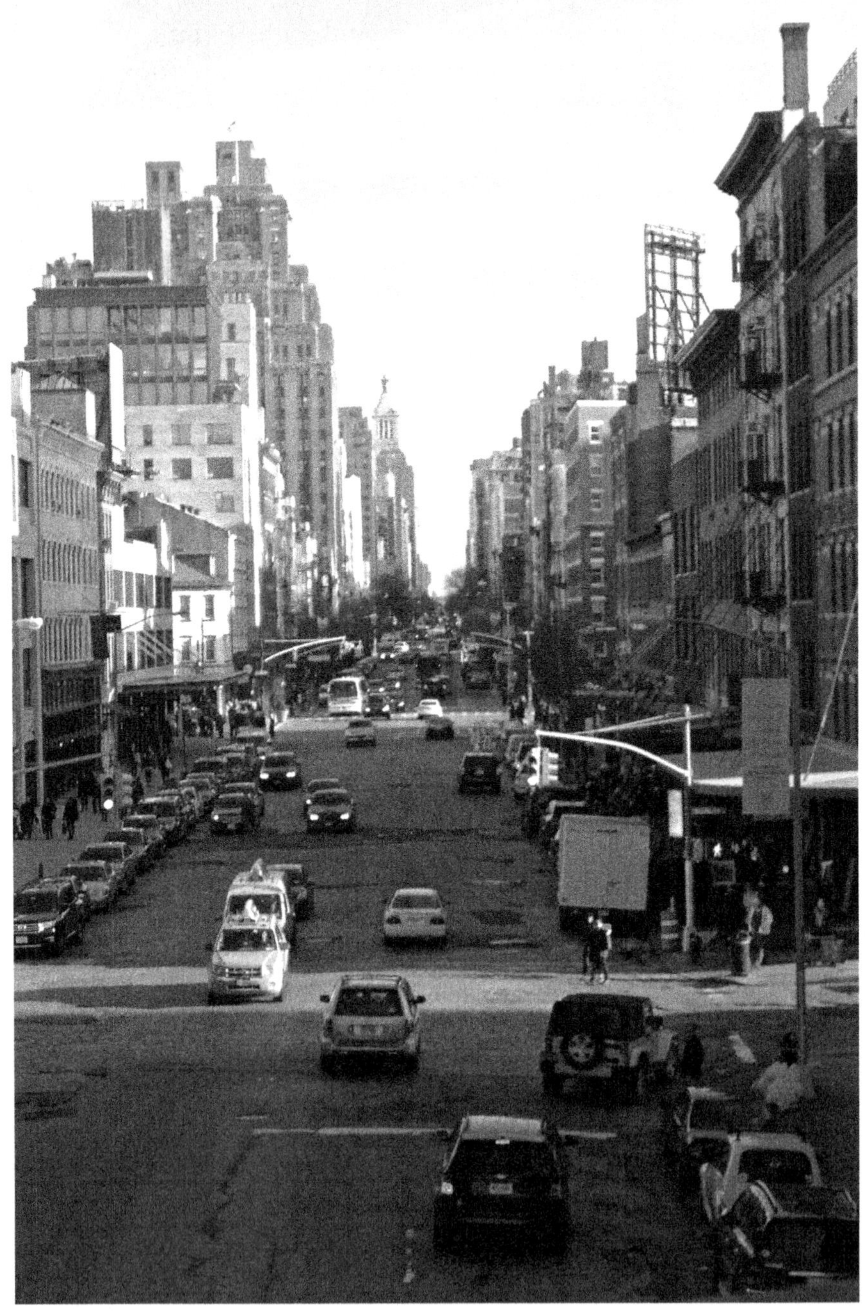

KELLY ESTOMO

BEING OKAY WITH NOT BEING OKAY

Think about breath,
the way it hitches when you're not okay.
Think about the exhale bumping into every dirty word collecting dust in your throat,
teeth finding knuckles to sink in so your nerves can give those words a painful message:
that your body doesn't want them there anymore.

Think about breath,
about someone else's,
how happy you are that they coexist in this timeframe with you.

My aunt's and uncle's dogs are my dogs too;
my cousins as much as their kids.
Both pant heavily, muzzle ajar and tongue hanging.
I'd like to think they're smiling and that their hearts are pumping too fast and too excited for their breath to catch up.
I'm so lucky.

Think about public speaking.

Speeches are a beast I can't tame with a shaky diaphragm.
Or maybe the monster is overthinking.
I present in sweaters to warm up wobbly arms and buffering sentences in rehearsed lineups.
Breath is too flighty,
and so are sparrows,
but an eagle soars.

Think about someone who's supposed to be close to you
dying.
Your breath is too steadily paced for this,
or did it stop?
You're worried regardless,
because family and friends are apologizing and you're wondering what for.

The passing comes second
to the guilt of not feeling as much as everyone expects you to.

Think of the streets of bodies
who exhale bits of their day at various seconds
but never at the same time.
Think about how 7 billion people's breaths will never align in pace,
and no matter how much they say we are one as a race
we cannot be one whole,
not this way.

Breathe first,
then think about the girl you put out of your head because you didn't know.
Now breathe out
because you know too much.
When the birds sing to themselves tomorrow morning,
you can groan loudly, but try and convince yourself that they're singing for you.

Think about your body heaving when you don't feel like breathing this time.
Think about your body wanting to breathe anyway.
Think about white blood cells ganging up on a virus breaking and entering into your system,
and how your entire being wants you to exist so bad,
how your body will fight for you when your heart and head gave up,
or how you breathe anyway.

Think about the armour you believe doesn't fit you anymore.
Now hold your breath...
and when the warzone in your head goes quiet,
don't think about the weights you can't lift,
or what you're missing,
or what to tweet next,
or who they're kissing.

When you're ready,
an exhale will pry your lips open just to escape.
And when you think about why you couldn't hold your breath,
it's everything in you saying you've got to,
you've got to,
you've got to.

MAHEK SHERGILL

IDYLLIC

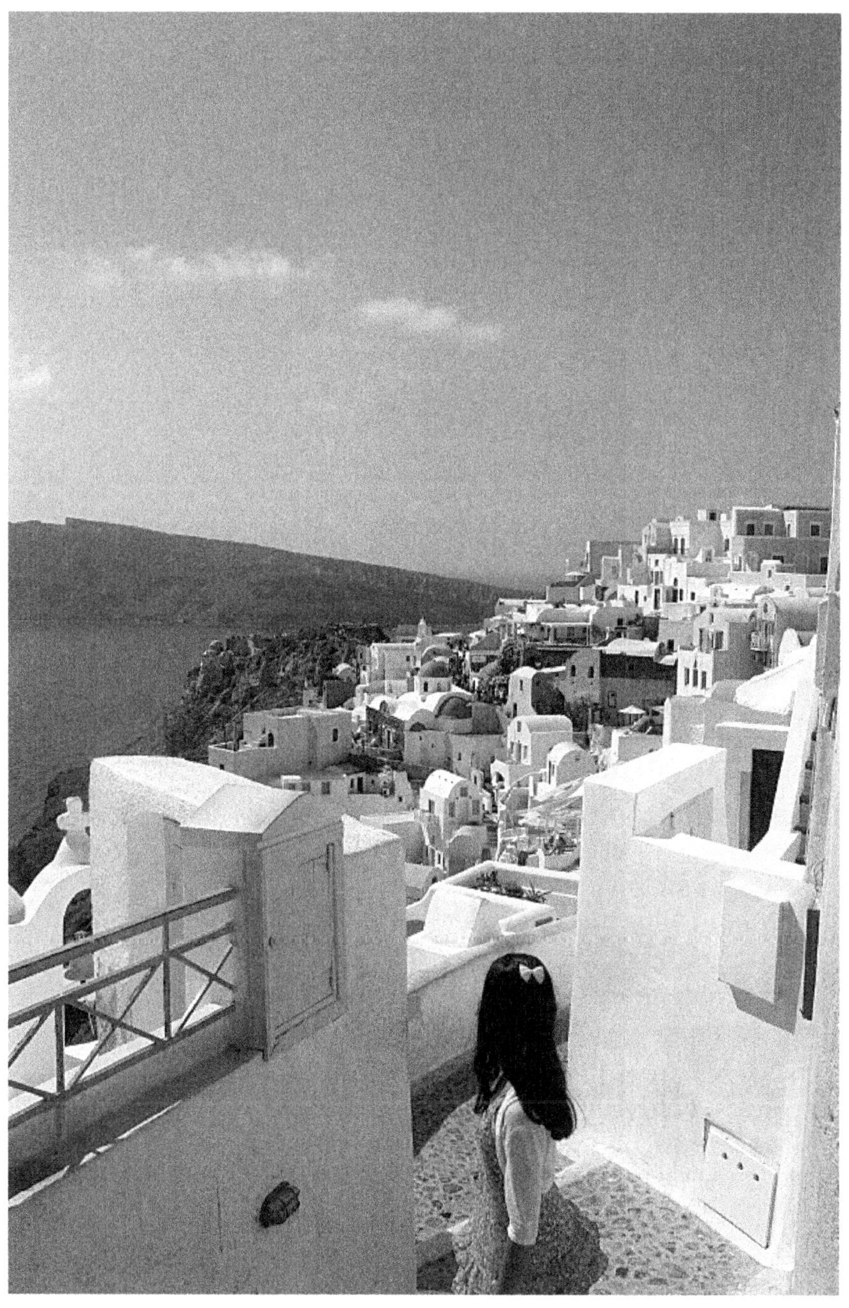

AFNAN NAEEM

LITTLE SOULS

We look up
at the crust of moon
planted in the starry plethora
of darkness.

A shade of its dull light
spills upon us
and makes us seemingless
little souls,
outlooking a wrathful world.

Amidst this blanket
of night sky,
your gaze jumps
from the shady canyon of
your heart

And lands among
the lofty lowlands of
my eyes,
catching my meek,
little soul.

Together, our rivers of
combustible blood ignite
two smiles of solace,
making our little souls
like stars—

Stars, on the verge of becoming
supernovas,
glistering the surrounding
blackness
of this wrathful world.

HARSHETHA SUNDAR

DARK REMINISCENCE

KATHRYN CHUNG

ANOTHER 10

To myself ten years ago,

If I remember correctly, my greatest fear was not turning out as I wanted. To look back and see failure and mistakes and missed opportunities. A heavy head, and an even heavier heart; I remember when growing up only meant comparing heights and finding love. I know my eyes are glassed with rose coloured lenses, short-sighted adolescence, and a touch of bittersweet nostalgia, but I remember you differently than you'd think. Let me tell you, these will be some of the happiest times in your life. Life will be hard, and I'm sorry to say it will only get harder. With you, I remember those hot summer days wasted away with cartoons and recess, with Gameboys and books. I remember the quiet innocence and trivial worries spent more on passing notes and less on passing grades. Trust me, I know you think the science fair is nothing to laugh at, but I know you'll manage. Even when you start the night before.

I know being ten is all about riding bikes and playing tag. I know it's about climbing the highest and doing cartwheels in the sand. I know it's about being a Pokemon Master and secretly bringing gum to school. You'll make incredibly stupid choices with a few good ones mixed in somewhere. I know you'll worry over school and grades, and even now, ten years later, I can say I understand your pain. I know your best friend is leaving next year, but it's nothing to worry about because you'll meet someone even more irreplaceable in the next grade. Please remember to love her always and stay close. Keep to your promise of staying best friends forever, even if I know you'll eventually break it.

I know high school seems like millions of years away, but trust me when I say it will come in the blink of an eye. Be prepared for some of the hardest years of growing up. You'll go through a big change, both on the inside and the outside. Like a miniature grenade, you'll be forced to decide what really matters in your life. Please remember to always have courage, and to always be kind, because when life is cruel, sometimes, this is all you'll have left. The first year will be difficult and lonely, but you'll find yourself attracting the most loyal, most amazing people you could ever deserve. Stick with them, and six years later they'll be more than just drinking buddies; they'll be the idiots you take on the world with.

I want you to remember all of life's lessons and all of your choices. I want you to remember the memories that stab you with raw nostalgia and rip open your insides. You'll be hit with pain and sadness and self-loathing. You'll cry, you'll fall, and you'll make so many mistakes that you'll lose count. Always remember that life happens. Yeah, you're an idiot who often makes the wrong choice, but you're a survivor, a fighter. You have friends and family, and alongside every single bad memory is a better one. You'll laugh with friends, roll down grassy hills, have snowball fights, and stay up late talking about everything and nothing. Despite your disbelief, you'll have a date to prom and pass your driving test. No matter how scary life gets, I want you to know you made it. You may think you've already passed the starting line, but you'll rethink that the night before your twentieth birthday. You'll be fine for another ten years, and on my thirtieth birthday, I'll tell you, you'll be fine for ten more.

I know that living without regrets is impossible, so I'll tell you to live happily instead. You've lived ten years, and you'll live ten more. After all, I'm here as proof that everything you did, all the efforts you took, all the mistakes you made were not in vain.

Let's live at least another eighty together,

Your twenty-year-old self

KRISTEN LORITZ

NO HOMO

Butt slapping, chest bumping and bear hugging are among the many peculiar rituals that athletes engage in. Yet some individuals feel compelled to utter "no homo" after a tush smack. Why? Because one must announce their heterosexuality before others question it; one fears these actions implicate judgment because *why else would you slap a butt? How gay of you.*

While some athletes thrive in intimate settings by sharing harmless expressions of endearment, routine, or comic relief, others question these practices and their homoerotic suggestiveness. Add a dash of youth, a dollop of hormones, and a pinch of sexuality, and this swirling mix often crafts an entrée of confusion, anxiety, and discomfort among many athletes. To stir the pot further, the ease of inscribing homosexual labels onto individual athletes parallels the practice of gendering sporting disciplines themselves.

Bronzer, hairspray, and rhinestones: feminized features of the figure skating world that strikingly differ from the average males' preferred attire. Both myself and my male teammate use all of these embellishments while competing. Yes, I even steal his hairspray too.

These effeminate practices set the discipline of figure skating up for feminized labels and consequently promotes homosexual identification with male athletes. This problematic view of sports may confuse your gaydar because although Lee skates and displays metrosexual mannerisms, easily confused for homosexual, he is identifiably straight.

Sexual stereotypes manifest misunderstanding, injustice, and alienation. My own fear of labels and orientation-based judgment brings me shame and self-disdain, but worse, I once questioned my own teammate, my faux-brother, my confidant, my best friend: homo or *no homo? Why did I even care?*

Navy knee-highs, white starchy shirts, and a burgundy plaid skirt: my "Jesus outfit," a teacher once said. These signifying articles identified me as a Catholic school girl: an *all-girls* Catholic school girl. Single-gendered class by day, followed by single-gendered skating practice at night: *all girls* practice.

The Catholic high school system grew out of notions developed by the Catholic church, including views that encompassed traditional hegemonic ideas of femininity: *heterosexual femininity.*

A lesbian at school? Where and who? Each rumour provoked curiosity, and each rumour subverted perceptions of my own identity. What did my peers think of my solely female oriented choices: ultra-feminine or secretly lesbian? Although neither label speaks to my case, Johnson & Kivel (2006) say that the labeling process begins and ends in the physicality of the sport, with the assumption that muscle equates to lesbianism (107)[4]. As a fairly active and muscular female teen, had I sent out the wrong message to my friends and society? Because of these crafted ideas surrounding heterosexual women, I questioned my identity and I questioned how one *should* be.

A heterosexual/homosexual binary in sports reduces athletes to their sexual orientation. *Gay?* some say. *That explains a lot.* To judge, measure, and assess an individual this way dilutes their credibility, expertise, and performance quality. These negative and diminishing thoughts draw their roots in institutionalization – including the hegemonic heterosexual ideas taught to me from an early age in the Catholic classrooms of my youth. Similarly, the narrow masculine – or feminine – characteristics that sporting disciplines promote presents a systemic problem that traditionally left two options for athletes: subject themselves to questioning and/or harassment, or suppress and remain silent about their sexualities. To stray in any way from heterosexuality threatens tradition; it threatens the stereotypes that have been used to construct sporting domains for hundreds of years.

While my own single-gendered choices appear to place my identity and sexuality into question, more serious labels lurk across the gender border.

Player and *womanizer* reflect masculine ideals of men who frequently engage with woman in a sexual or suggestive way. So what labels await the sole male participating in a predominantly female sport? A player? I think not.

Meet my Ukrainian-Filipino teammate, Lee: a man with an endless supply of girls who gawk at and swoon over him. Lee may garner attention for his sole-male status on a female team, but this attention has also lead to questions of his sexuality.

Tall, thin, and talented, Lee entered the competitive synchronized skating stream five years ago as the first male accepted onto the Canadian National Team, NEXXICE Senior. Months passed and teammates whispered. We all questioned Lee's sexuality. We all anticipated 'the truth' to surface. We all waited for him to speak. We all judged from afar.

"We'll crack him," the girls would say. "Maybe he'll confess." Confess what? Confession suggests violation, disobedience and error. Yet no matter what my church, school or peers teach and believe, *homosexuality is not a sin.*

Lee's sexual choices do not impact his performance as a skater, nor should they change the way my teammates and I view him. Mysteries, secrets, and uncertainties often prompt speculation. But speculation easily grows from innocent to intrusive. Perhaps some teammates, coaches, and parents would simply feel comfortable if they knew Lee's orientation, because comfort for many of these girls, including myself, arrived in a pristine Catholic package. Comfort arrived from an institution that reinforces the binary between homosexual and heterosexual; an institution that celebrates the destruction of the 'Other' orientation and celebration of one. It is why even five years later, guilt bubbles within me knowing that I participated in exchanging thoughts and words about Lee that I could never tell him; the cruel assumptions of a teenage mind.

No homo should become a declaration of support, saying NO to homophobia, no to questioning and no to those who embed division in sport, in society and within us all.

LUCIA SALVATI

LIGHT AT THE END OF THE TUNNEL

DANICA DY

ON THE FIRST DAY OF SCHOOL

On the first day of school,

I woke up early to the song of birds and sound of the kettle. The sun was dawning on a new day, a new chapter. I hopped out of bed and ran down the stairs. Mom helped me button my shirt and buckle my shoes. She packed my bag with notebooks, crayons, and a juice box. I anxiously waited by the window, butterflies in my stomach, and finally a big yellow bus rolled into the driveway. Mom opened the front door, and I raced down the front steps toward the bus, only to turn back with hesitation to realize I didn't know what school would be like. I turned around to see Mom standing in the doorway, her eyes welling up with tears. I didn't understand why. I walked back toward the porch and together we walked toward the bus hand-in-hand.

On the first day of school,

I lay in bed waiting for the right moment to get up and face the day. Mom yelled at me from downstairs, and today there were no song birds or kettles. I rolled out of bed and made my way down the stairs. I dressed myself, tied my laces, and packed my bag with binders and pencils. There was no more colour. It seemed much heavier than I remembered. I dreaded the top of the hour when the next bus would arrive, but surely it came. There were still butterflies in my stomach. I opened the door and made my way toward the stop. It wasn't a shining yellow bus anymore, but a city bus spattered with dust, filled with other people off to start their day. I turned back to find my mom, with greying hair, in the doorway. Her eyes were welling up with tears. I now understood why, but the bus was almost at the stop and there was no turning back. I walked to the stop alone.

On the first day of school,

For the first time, I woke up in a bed that wasn't my own. Across the room was a person I had only met a few days ago. Mom had helped me move into my dorm. I pulled off my covers and made my way to the bathroom. I dressed myself, fixed my hair, and put on make-up as my mind raced in preparation to face the day. I made my way down the hall, around foreign buildings, down walkways that had be trod on by hundreds of other students who, like me, felt butterflies on their first day of school. For the first time, on the first day of school, I wasn't leaving from my own house. For the first time, there was no Mom. Though I could not turn back to see her standing in the doorway this time, I knew that somewhere she was looking at a clock, with salt and pepper hair, thinking of me.

She would question why time had passed, why it had gone so quickly and why I had to grow up. She will sit, watching the hour, as I had done invariably over the years and think *I wish I could hold your hand the way I held hers before she left for her first day of school.*

IOANA PITU

ILLUSION

ABEERA SHAHID

MEDLEY

Born and raised in a country of desperation,
Born and raised in a household of beauty.

A change across oceans,
A spark beyond descriptive emotions,
A journey to call my own.

Challenges arose.
From language barriers to cultural barriers,
Stereotypes hold us in an envelope,
With the whole story buried beneath.

Little girl, nine years old
Left it all behind
New school
New people
New friends
New Her.

Little girl no more,
She knows herself,
Stereotypes are not always lies,
But the incomplete truth.
Open the envelope,
Complete the story.

They ask me who I am,
I am you, I say.
Silent stares.
Why is it so hard to believe that when you meet me, you have left a part of you with me?
Don't worry, I'll take care of it.

Even when I have nothing, *I'll give*;
Even when I have one piece of bread, *I'll share*;
Even if you show up unexpected, *I'll welcome you*;
Because I live in a small house with a huge heart.

Ubuntu: I am because of you.
I am because of you.

CHELSEA TAO

A PARTICULAR DROWNING

say, catch me a river
end up unafraid and far into the
depths of the next breeding.
The greatest fact about tomorrow
is that it never dies the way it is supposed to
a shifting ghost, a viable trail of phantom
handprints pressed into the midnight hour
growing visible with the caution of escape.

An unquenchable thirst comes from your mouth
I can feel it
dancing on the tips of your canines threatening
to drop with ripeness at any time
but know that this is not poison spread over your tongue.
With your age, remember tomorrow
how it never dies the way it is supposed to
instead a chameleon, a malleable spine,
a weeknight alone and under the watch of
God-infused refusal
or both.

This is a particular drowning
under your bullet-filled tapestry of skin
there is no place left for mercy.
Your hands never come close to my self-discovery

placed like summer hills on top of each
other and sweating the future into the walls
as if there is still some good in them.
Under you, a petulant corruption wrapped in
nationalist silk
Under me, a poem to be punished and burned
with the wind.

This is a particular drowning
I don't recall the water, only a wave
goodbye, as if a shake of the
Earth could rupture me from you.
I don't recall the blood, only a hospital room,
your body a cloak around my infancy
already apologizing for the consequence of love.

GISELLE SALDANHA

BASILICA OF SAINTE-ANNE-DE-BEAUPRE DANS QUEBEC

ADIL KHAN

WAITING

Every day, I sit here on my porch, in my old rocking chair. Being a lonely old man, this is all I have left. My neighbors say that I scare their children. But they don't know my story.

I was a part of a poor family in Germany. My father could never find work. When we were told that we could take a train to a better place and have a better life, we didn't even think twice. Everyone on the train was very nice. But when the train didn't stop for many days, we started to get worried.

When we finally stopped, the camp looked nothing like what we were promised. There were huge black spiders on red flags, looming over us. My father and I were separated from my mother and sisters. We never saw them again. I asked all my friends from the train where they were. They never answered.

All of us men were put in a line. They asked us our age. Everyone under 16 was put in a separate line. I knew something bad was going to happen to them. I was only 15.

When the guard asked me my age, I confidently answered, "17." He eyed me suspiciously. Sweat trickled down the back of my neck.

"Move along," he said.

I asked one of the scary men in uniforms where my mother and sisters were. I wanted to see them again. He looked over towards a dark building, where I could hear painful wails of agony. He pointed at the smoke coming out of the building. The vulgar stench of something burning made me want to gag. He said, "Some of them over there, and bits of them over there." Only later did I understand. I wasn't going to see them again.

When my father fell ill from all the hard work he was being forced to do, they showed him no mercy. He was taken away from me, and the others had to hold me back. I wanted to kill them all that day. I didn't need to ask what happened to him. I wasn't the same child I was when I lost my mother.

One day, we could tell that something was wrong. The guards seemed worried or scared. They were in a hurry, but I had no idea about what. I was sure that the older men knew, but they said I was too young. Something about a war, Allies, and a Fuhrer. But if these Allies were scaring the people who took my family from me, I was waiting for them to come save me.

I had no idea what these horrible people gained from this. What could they hope to accomplish from torturing us? Every day, I was forced to spend endless hours working hard jobs. What was the point of smashing rocks in the blazing hot sun all day? We got little, if any, food to eat. I could soon see the changes in my body from lack of food. My bones soon started showing; my ribs visible underneath my ragged clothes. This was not how my life was supposed to end; I was only a teenager. I shouldn't find it a challenge just to stand. Soon, I got used to the feeling of absolute hunger and thirst, but most of the others weren't so lucky.

As time passed, I lost all hope. I stopped counting the days, for the numbers had become too high. One of the days I remember in particular was when I woke up to the sound of guns blazing. Not that that was new; we were used to it. But for the first time, it seemed like the guns weren't being fired at us. I watched with a smile that I could barely manage as my captors fled like the cowards they were. For once, they had to fight against those who could fight back, unlike the millions of innocent that now rot in the dirt.

The Allies had come, and the storm that we had endured for so long had finally subsided. This all happened because one man didn't like who my people were. If he had known any of us, would this not have happened? I was told that he was brought to justice, but all is not well. What I had see, could never go away. It haunted me in my sleep, and I knew that I could not stay there anymore. So I moved to America to escape my nightmares.

So now I just sit here on my porch, waiting for the only thing someone with nothing can wait for.

NATHAN DUONG

SUBTERRANEO

JORDAN CURRIE

BITTER

I'm bitter.
Not in the way that black coffee warms the inside of your body with every gentle sip.
Not in the way that dark chocolate melts on the roof of your tongue.
Not in the way that wine swirls around on your palette and loosens your inhibitions.
I am not the good-tasting kind of bitter.

This is how I lash out
when I am not met with what I want.
It sounds selfish, and God knows it is.
I'm not quite rotten yet,
but my insides are no longer as sweet as sugar;
maybe they never were,
and suddenly I'm not the ripe piece of fruit I try to be.

If I was a fruit, my peel would not be thick,
much like my skin.
I am not something edible;
I am not something desirable.

Most people prefer sweet.
Bitter can challenge you, but sweetness
always tastes familiar, always tastes like home.
I do not remind anyone of what "home" is.

Just know that I am sorry.
I want too much sweet, too much to the point
that I get achingly sick from desiring it;
a child on Halloween night.
My bitterness throws me back;
reminds me of who I really am
and how I could never handle that much sweetness anyways.
It's not like I have the ability to obtain it, anyway.

I don't mean to be this person who derives off of being sour.
Sometimes, seeing the sweetness in others unleashes the bitter in me.
Just know that I am sorry.
My bitterness is not something I can always control.
When you're deprived of sugar for so long, bitterness can feel like a substitute sweetener.

TANISHA MEHTA

WE ARE WILD THINGS

i. i plant flowers in my throat
in hopes they'll grow into my skull
i want to see my eyelashes fall out
let petals push through their abandoned holes

ii. everything i want to say is tangled in the roots
but the buds are yellow and shining
they tilt towards the sun and close when it's not around
i want to live in the light

iii. it's funny that you don't have your own set of flowers
i swear i feel thorns every time you touch me

iv. there are weeds wrapping around my neck
they need the sun more than i do
green leaves have covered mine

v. you are an invasive species
but our stems are tangled
and i can't let go

vi. please let me go

GISELLE SALDANHA

IMPERFECTION IS BEAUTY

BRITTANY BEHESHTI

THE LIBERTY OF CHOICE

I watched quietly from the bushes. My long hair tickled my calf as I knelt down, still as stone. The forest felt calm and cool. I shifted my weight smoothly to my right foot, careful not to move the green leaves that concealed me. The deer stood ten feet away, poised majestically as though it came from a myth. Its brown fur was sleek and smooth, and its muscles were tensed as it bent its head to eat the nearest bush. I skillfully nocked my bow and steadied my breathing.

I readjusted my stance and pulled the arrow back to my cheek. All the muscles in my body were tense as I held my breath. As I considered letting go to seal the creature's fate, I saw movement by the creature's feet. A baby. It couldn't have been older than a week. Arrow still poised, I had to make a choice, but for me it wasn't much of a choice. I lowered my bow. The other women would patronize me for coming home empty handed, but I would not come home with dinner and leave that baby to die alone. I took a step back, and the leaves and twigs crunched under my feet. The mother's head jolted up, ears perked in attention. Her nose was high in the air; I could tell she sensed me. She pushed her baby to its feet, and they quickly moved away. I stood and released my breath. I turned and headed back to camp.

"How was your first hunt alone?" Claria asked softly. I looked up at her from my seat. She was as tall as most of us. Her broad shoulders and thick muscles were proof of her high status as a warrior, but her gentle voice was what makes her different than most of the women here. The Amazon women lived on a simple philosophy: women can be just as strong as men. I've seen the way women are treated in the Greek cities, and I couldn't fathom why they would stay. There was no liberty.

"I tracked a doe. But I couldn't bring myself to do it." She looked at me with pity. "It was a mother," I said, knowing it wouldn't make a difference. In our society becoming a warrior was all that was important, and leaving food behind, for any reason, was seen as weakness.

"You are an extremely talented new warrior, but your weak heart is holding you back. One day you will have to kill something, Kenzia." She said it politely, but the words still filled me with dread. All the women here were trained in combat from a young age, and all the people in our city could be battle ready if necessary, but how could I defend my family if I couldn't even kill a deer?

Suddenly, the horn sounded. The guard rushed to Claria. "The Greeks," the guard huffed. "They're headed this way. It's more than just a few. Claria, this is an army." Without a word, we were all moving fast. Horses were mounted, and bows were collected. We moved swiftly as a single unit.

My bow was slung across my back along with a quiver full of arrows. The hooves hit the forest floor hard as we flew over the terrain. We slowed as we approached the army. Claria gave the signal, and we silently nocked our arrows. The wind went calm for a split second as hundreds of arrows drove through the trees and mercilessly sliced through the armour of the front line. The attack was stealthy and quick, leaving the Greeks in a quick moment of panic.

I urged my horse forward towards these men. Nocking my bow again, I shot another arrow. It landed on its mark, and a strong warrior fell from his horse. My face was cold as stone. I realized there's a difference: killing an innocent mother or killing an armed soldier here to hurt my family. My arms moved on their own accord as the muscles flexed and released, leaving wounded in my wake. My body ducked quickly to dodge an arrow heading straight for my head, but my horse wasn't so lucky. He was hit in the chest and reared quickly out of fear and pain. I was thrown off the horse, and I landed hard on my side. My body ached as I urged myself to my feet. My left leg burned as I added more and more weight to it.

Unsure about what to do next, I moved towards the yelling. I began to pick up speed when all of a sudden, I was knocked down by a strong arm. I fell to the ground with a thud. The Greek man stood above me. He had a pointed jaw and a long face. He winced in pain as he took a step towards me. I looked down from his face to see his lower torso soaked in blood. His arm held his right side defensively while the other hand held a club also covered in blood. He weakly raised his club, and I knew I needed to act. Now.

Quick as a whip, I rolled onto my back and shot my leg out, aiming for his wound. My foot hit its mark, and, despite the protective hand, the man screamed in pain, dropping his club in the process. It gave me the chance to scramble up. My eyes glanced frantically for my bow lying limply a few feet away. I darted out and snatched it off the ground. Within seconds, I had my bow nocked and aimed at his throat. He froze eyes wide with fear. We were both breathing heavily. His mannerisms changed completely as he hung his head down in defeat.

That's when the adrenaline stopped.

He stood as defenseless as the deer, just a man fighting someone else's war. He was wounded, tired, and weaponless. I knew I should have killed him. I saw his blood-covered club. He was not as innocent as the doe, and yet... The moment seemed to have lasted forever. Slowly, I made my choice. I lowered my bow. This wasn't who I am. I was not a ruthless killer.

The man looked up and saw my weapon lowered. His hand instantly reached for his belt. He pulled his dagger out and hurled it into the air. After seeing the knife slice through the air, I didn't see anything else. It was all spinning and blotchy.

"Stupid woman," I heard through the noise. There was a searing pain in my chest. Compassion is what killed me: my compassion and his ruthlessness.

JANE JOMY

YOU'RE TOO PRETTY TO BE SINGLE

UMER AMJAD

THE TALE OF A LIFE

A life was born one day
A life not black and white, but grey
Not purely happy, not just sad, such is the way
That our journey must be; come what may

This life was meant to suffer, be in misery, and feel pain.
This human life, filled with ice, fire, and rain,
It asks itself, "Why must I do this? Is all in vain?
Why must I ache? Why must I strain?"
The mortals think life bane,
Saying, "Those who disagree must be insane."

"Fear, hate, sorrow, cries,
Is this where my destiny lies?"
The man asks himself, so unwise.
One day, this life meets a Spirit of Light, with disbelieving eyes
He asks it, "Why does anyone live, if everyone dies?"
"This is not something I can answer easily," the Spirit replies.
"To show you the truth, I must take you somewhere. Rise!"

The mortal followed the mentor, unsure what he would see.
They went into a place freezing and shadowy.
"O Spirit, where art thou taking me?"
"A place unfit for life, a place unfit for thee."
"But cannot I stay somewhere warm? I do not understand clearly;
Perhaps this is to show me that life is cold and brutal, could it be?"
"Do not believe that yet. Let go of preconceptions. Break the chains of destiny. Become free!"

They continued their adventure, the human becoming hopeless.
"I do not feel better. Like life, this all feels pointless."
They went into a place burning, blindingly radiant, lifeless.
"You said you wanted warmth. Do you see the consequence of your bias?"

"Spirit, I do not understand. Of all this, what is the purpose?"
"Do you not perceive the contrast? Let yourself see from the heart, not the iris.
Do not believe life is so black and white, for how can it be? Break the chains of destiny! Become boundless!

"You asked me why we live if it is so punishing.
You asked me why we die if life has a meaning.
Just as Light cannot exist without Darkness, so too life is filled with happiness and suffering
Only in the cold, you realized you needed heating.
Then, in the fire, still, you were quick to fleeing.
Unable to handle extremes; a midpoint you were needing
Because with winter and summer, there is autumn and spring.
One needs to experience both justice *and* evil to keep their heart beating.

"Without hardships, how could you know the blessing of ease?
How could you know the joy of a smile without the frown of disease?
Do you see now why Life is not a breeze?
Both love and hate are needed to develop, to evolve, to seize
The chance to understand others, the chance to cause a change, the chance to please.
We can only make the world better by bettering ourselves first, so do not sleaze.
We can only better ourselves by seeing all the world's villainies."

The man asked, in denial, "But why do we face love and hate?
Why does our acceptance matter if all is in our Fate?"
"Our conflicting sides of Hell and Heaven give us the power to decide our own destination," answered the Spirit, frustrated.
"Remember your path will not always be straight
But no matter how dark or difficult it gets, you must believe you *can* bear the weight.
Both friends and enemies you will encounter; no matter what, exonerate.
Unshackle destiny's seeming restraints; all *is* meant to be, but the *choice* of it is yours; differentiate.

"Answers to your many questions have been given; what else do you inquire?"
"Please tell me, O Spirit to achieve these goals, what need I acquire?"
"Let your fiery heart melt the ice of cold desire.
Become Water, full of life, easy to flow with, able to quench rage's fire.
Become Wind, a soft breeze, invulnerable to hate, gentle, but able to inspire.
Become Earth, a firm foundation of truth, of unshakable valour to admire.
Become Light, a beacon of hope, a shining guide in the Dark, a spark to aspire."

And so, the Spirit bid farewell, leaving the man with his life illuminate.d
He lived the rest of it giving up himself. "I can help you," he would say to all souls, unimpeded.
Alas, a day came when the skies wept; the life faced its mortality, but pleaded,
"Do not let me die yet! I have failed, O Spirit, I could not save humanity... if only I had never conceded."
"No! 'To know even *one* life has breathed easier because you have lived. This is to have *succeeded!*[6]'
Your time as human may be done, but you will return when you are needed, O Enlightened One."

One day, another life of Dark and Light was born again.
A man, but changed anew as a Spirit of Light, appeared then.
Recently evolved, still reminiscing of its humanity, the Spirit consoled the life, "I can help you, friend
This is a new beginning, not the end."

RAMINDER DHANOA

INTO THE WOODS

The silence was the first thing I noticed. A shroud of stillness had crept itself into me, delving into my psyche and making me aware of every breath, step, and heartbeat my body produced among the myriad of towering observers. The glow of moss-covered branches against the evening sun created a peculiar aura of bright, cheery benevolence despite the ever-so steady deepening of the sun's colour.

I knew I should return quickly. But something about facing the lofty, shackling responsibilities on my shoulders made me want to push them even further away. I had to clear my head. I walked further into the untamed swath of wooded outgrowth, the peace of the forest feeding something deep and primordial within me.

As I strode forward, I thought back to a simpler time, when the joy of friendship greeted me behind every corner. When my world was smaller, safer, and overflowing with laughter and life. When I awoke each day with a passion to be my very best, instead of feeling like life was just one long string of disappointment, loss, and dampening of every impassioned impulse I had ever felt in my life. The warmth and familiar hope that nostalgia once brought quickly withered into a malicious regret. *Where did everything go wrong? Why am I so far from where I want to be?*

I pushed the thoughts away fervently. My issues weren't actually real, I told myself. They were all just in my head. But that was exactly the problem.

The dark silhouette of the stark, towering pines among the surrounding mountains stood watching, brooding even, as the wind shook them into a frenzy. The cool evening air felt welcome as the scent of earth and pine weaved itself into an ever self-complementing embrace. In the loneliness of the woods, a peculiar sensation took root in my chest cavity. The isolation created an absence of the drowning sensation I had felt among others; my mind was free to think and exist as any sort of entity it wished to be. Unfortunately, it didn't always play to my best interests.

An emptiness welled up inside me like a contaminated spring leaking its poison up into the ground. Only it was an empty, debilitating type of sadness, the kind that you hid away in the darkest recesses of yourself and that you didn't even know existed until you feel it festering within. I desperately fought off the melancholy, brushing it off and resisting its seductive, gravitational power until eventually I gave in to the relentless pull of the sadness.

The thoughts swirled around me, picking apart the bit of sanity I had left like a pack of shrieking, bloodcurdling ravens. *You'll never be understood. You'll never find a place where you belong. Everything you do is meaningless. You'll never be good enough. You'll never be beautiful. You're trapped. There is no way out.* The irrevocable, disseminating stench of my thoughts was only made worse by their inability to float away. The bell jar enclosed in my mind only made them develop further, deeper, and emptier. I strode into a clearing of thickets and euonymus bushes, hoping to catch a glimpse of the sunset I knew was coming.

I looked up, saw the dark outline of mountains against the warm orange sky, and was startled into awareness of the sheer size of the landscape. The sublime washed away at my worries. This was what I'd been missing. The impending sense of colossal, indestructible and infinite power before me was a validation of my own insignificance against the supreme beauty and awe of the universe.

As the light faded from the clouds, I turned back whence I came, eager to make my way back before night crept up into the shadows of the landscape. Darkness descended swifter than I anticipated, and I rushed into a jog. Feeling an uncanny unease at the fringes of my consciousness, my eyes fluttered about, imagining movements among the reed bushes in the distance. A far-off howl was heard, though it very well could have been in my imagination.

The pines creaked as a gale blew down into the valley. The urge to return to familiarity, the fear of the unknown, and the unknowingness of what was to come should I cease to move forward propelled me back into the maze of cedars that had greeted me hours earlier.

I couldn't quite describe how I felt. The serenity and raw purity of nature had certainly cleared my head, but I still couldn't shake the dull, relentless sense of apathy that remained within me. If it weren't for the primeval fear of the untamed leading me onward, I probably could've lay among the bulrushes and grasses for as long as my body allowed.

That was when, of course, I realized the unfamiliarity in my surroundings. Trying not to incite myself into a panic, I leapt ahead, dark-chestnut trunk after trunk, until eventually I began to feel my inherent cynicism attract itself back to me like a magnet. I couldn't allow myself to question my sense of direction lest I end up even more lost. I didn't exactly know the way, but that didn't stop me from moving forward.

Trusting myself onwards, I trudged through the duskiness, meandering into the unfamiliar grey of the night.

CHRIS YAO

COUPLE OF THE EAST DON RIVER

RACHEL TRAN

THE UNKNOWN OBSERVER

What am I?
I am the earth, the sky, and living things in-between.
I am old, older than you;
Older than your parents, grandparents;
Older than the combined ages of many descendants.

I have seen sinners with my very eyes,
And the bottomless depths behind the eyes of those
Who truly should be feared.
I have witnessed real acts of kindness,
The simplest of gestures from hearts of glittering lights.
The fog that is my mind fails to recount all the sights
That have crossed paths with me,
But I will forever remember
The creature I once was.
Ambitious, greedy, fearful, lonely, strong.
A lover, an enemy, a believer, a traitor,
A being with more regrets than his days of valour.

When my line was about to be cut, I smiled
Because the world was going to be better without me.
But the fates play games; they never let you win.
They said to me, in voices of those I loathed,
"May your body rot and your black soul thrive
Within the giants that will never cease to survive."

What am I?
I am a spirit moulded into
The lonely shield of some useless tree
With bark as white as the angel that guides
Those drowning in the hungriest of tides.

I will always be an unknown observer,
And I am now at peace.

RYAN CHU

FRACTURE

I heard they found you crumpled up in a dirty alleyway. You should have seen it. Mother was clawing at your door; the doctors had to hold her down as she sobbed and screamed your name. She begged them to bring you back, to give you a second chance, because she believed with all her heart that you deserved one.

She locked herself in her room for three days. I didn't do anything. I didn't think it was worth the effort.

Do you remember the night when we went camping in the woods? I told you that I wanted to become an astronaut when I grew up so that I could swim among the stars. You laughed at me, called me crazy, but you said that you would have wanted to do the same.

That moment remains vivid, but the rest of my memories are bleak and vague. Nothing but a slideshow stuck on repeat; washed-out snapshots of you throwing glass and kissing cigarettes.

What happened to you? I ask myself every day, but I'm no closer to the answer than I was on that night when Mother's screams rang through the powder-white halls.

They say that some people find their life's answers at the bottom of a beer bottle.

I hope you found yours.

IBRAHIM ISSA

REWIND

TRAM NGUYEN

BOY KING OF THE FIELD

There once was a boy
Who crawled in my arms of grass
Clung onto my leafy tendrils
And basked in my summer sun

The winds came and carried him away
Toasting and singeing the ends of my leaves
Crusting and drying my skin
Winter waited my withering

Yellow flowers blotched throughout
Seizing the green grass' buds
The little boy returned
He was no longer little

With a crown of my leaves and twigs adorning his head
Hours he spent lying beneath my shade
Saying he loved everything I was
And everything his father wasn't

He loved me when I flourished
Left me when I iced
Summers went by as I rolled with the wind
I missed the boy

He came back one day
With newly etched ridges and wear on his face
His father had died and he told me he was sorry
As an army of acid machines barricaded my skin

He told them to come
They took everything he loved of me
And cut off my branches
Plucked off my grasses

He replaced me with metal monstrosity
Butterflies unfurled furiously from my grasp
Never dawdling in my presence again
I was nothing more than cold-faced cement

There once was a boy
Who learned to love a field.
His father told him that to love is to destroy,
And so he did.

JANE WANG

YESTERDAY

I was the rising sun
I was the bright new day
I was the breath of hope
I was the gentle rain

I was the crackling flame of a campfire surrounded by friends
I was the gentle lapping of waves on the beach
I was the curve of a rainbow just before it starts to bend
I was the softness of a lamb, a clear pastel peach

I was the enthusiasm of a puppy going out for a walk
I was the childlike wonder that never stopped
I was naïve optimism, I was the intensity of a hawk
I was a firecracker waiting to pop
I was, I was, I was

REFERENCES

[1]George, M. (2005). Making Sense of Muscle: The Body Experiences of Collegiate Women Athletes. *Sociological Inquiry*, 75(3), 317-345.

[2]Goldman, A. (2014, April 25). There Are Now 'Anti-Thigh Gap' Jeans. *Women's Health.*

[3]Gueren, C. (2013, Dec 19). More Proof That the "Thigh-Gap Trend" Is Ridiculous. *Women's Health.*

[4]Johnson, C., & Kivel, B. (2006). Chapter 7: Gender, sexuality and queer theory in sport. In Aitchison, C. (Eds.), *Sport and Gender Identities: Masculinities, Femininities and Sexualities* (pp. 93-105).

[5]McNamara, (2014, Feb 22). Athletes pay no mind to 'gap'; the powerful quads on the women at the Sochi games illustrate the beauty in strength. Take that, thigh gap. *Los Angeles Times.*

[6]Ralph Waldo Emerson (1803-1882) American Essayist and Poet

ACKNOWLEDGEMENTS

The *Mississauga Youth Anthology: Volume III* was made possible through the generous support of several community partners and the commitment of the Ink Movement Mississauga team.

Thank you to the Art Gallery of Mississauga, and in particular, our mentor, Tina Chu, for their continued support throughout the year, working with us to realize success in each and every project. As well, thank you to the Mississauga Arts Council and the City of Mississauga for their ceaseless support to Ink Movement. Thank you to Samuel, Son & Co. Limited for the generous financial donation, and thank you to Cheryl Antao-Xavier and her team at In Our Words Inc. for publishing the anthology.

A huge thank you to the entire Ink Movement Mississauga team: Ahmad Younes, Amy Kwong, Ani Srikanth, Arisha Shoaib, Ashton Mathias, Baljeet Bhella, Chelsea Tao, Danielle Dy, Farida Rahman, Fatima Hasan, Haris Khalid, Inaara Panjwani, Inori Khan, Jane Wang, Jessica Myles, Jessica Feng, Kathy Hu, Meera Divakaran, Muhammad Haris, Murtuza Rajkotwala, Prachir Pasricha, Prasiddha Parthasarathy, Qurat Dar, Sadia Sheikh, Sara Wasim, Sarena Daljeet, Sianne Kuang, Simi Abreo, Tahreem Alvi, Tanisha Mehta, Tenaaz Irani, Uswa Zahoor, and Vaibhav Yadaram. A special thanks to Maxwell Tran, Ink Movement's Founder and Executive Director, for the constant inspiration and support. Thank you, team, for the countless hours we spent in the brainstorming, planning, promotion, selecting, and editing stages of the anthology. I couldn't have asked for a better group of passionate and motivated youth to work with.

It has been an 'ink'redible experience putting together this anthology. Thank you, Mississauga, for making our dreams come alive.

Until next time,

Cynthia Feng